Bezoar

and Other Unsettling Stories

T0025340

Bezoar

and Other Unsettling Stories

GUADALUPE NETTEL

translated by
Suzanne Jill Levine

Seven Stories Press
New York • Oakland

Seven Stories Press
140 Watts Street
New York, NY 10013
www.sevenstories.com

College professors and high school and middle school teachers may order free examination copies of Seven Stories Press titles. To order, visit www.sevenstories.com, or send a fax on school letterhead to (212) 226-1411.

Book design by Jon Gilbert

Library of Congress Cataloging-in-Publication Data

Names: Nettel, Guadalupe, 1973- author. | Levine, Suzanne Jill, translator.
Title: Bezoar : and other unsettling stories / Guadalupe Nettel ;
    translated from the Spanish by Suzanne Jill Levine.
Description: First English-language edition. | New York : Seven Stories
    Press, 2019. | "Title of the original Spanish edition: Pétalos y otras
    historias incómodas"
Identifiers: LCCN 2019023442 | ISBN 9781609809584 (paperback) | ISBN
9781609809591 (ebk)
Classification: LCC PQ7298.424.E76 A2 2019 | DDC 863/.7--dc23
LC record available at https://lccn.loc.gov/2019023442

Printed in the USA.

9 8 7 6 5 4 3 2 1

Contents

Ptosis
7

Through Shades
17

Bonsai
21

The Other Side of the Dock
43

Petals
61

Bezoar
75

Ptosis

My father's job, like many in this city, is parasitic. A photographer by trade, he would have starved to death—and with him the whole family—if not for Dr. Ruellan's generous offer, which, besides a decent salary, gave him the chance to focus his unpredictable inspiration on one mechanical task, with no major complications. Dr. Ruellan, the best eyelid surgeon in Paris, operates in the Hôpital des Quinze-Vingts, and his clientele is inexhaustible. Some patients would rather wait a year for an appointment with him than opt for a doctor of less renown. Before performing surgery on any given patient, our benefactor requests two sets of photographs. The first consists of five close-ups—eyes open and closed—as a record of their pre-operation condition. The second is done after surgery, once the incision has healed. Which is to say, no matter how satisfied our clients are with our work, we see them only twice in their lifetimes. Although on occasion the doctor will make a mistake—no one is perfect, not even him. One eye turns out more closed than the other, or maybe too open. Then the person comes back and we take a new set of photos, which costs them another three hundred euros, since my father has no hand in medical errors. Despite what you might think, eyelid surgery is very common and is performed for numerous reasons, starting with the ravages of age—the vanity of people who can't stand its signs on their faces. But there are also car accidents, which often disfigure passengers, explosions, fires, and other kinds of unforeseen events. The skin of an eyelid is unexpectedly delicate.

At our studio, near Place Gambetta, my father has hung some of the photos he took when he was young: a medieval bridge, a Romany hanging clothes out to dry beside her trailer, or an outdoor sculpture in the Luxembourg Gardens, which won him a youth prize in the city of Rennes. It's enough to see them to know that, in some distant past, the old man had talent. My father hangs more recent works as well: the face of a beautiful little boy who died in Dr. Ruellan's operating room (a complication during the anesthesia), his whole body shining on the table, bathed in a very bright, almost celestial light coming in at an angle from one of the windows.

I started working in the studio at fifteen, when I decided to leave school. My father needed an assistant and enlisted me for his team. I then learned the trade of a medical photographer specializing in ophthalmology. Although, as time went on, I gradually took charge of the office work, including accounting. I rarely go out to the city or countryside in search of a scene to inspire my fickle lens. On walks, I usually leave my camera behind, either because I forget it or because I'm afraid of losing it. I'll admit that even so, while walking the streets or the hallways of some building, I often have the sudden urge to take a picture, not of landscapes or bridges as my old man once did, but of some atypical eyelid I happen to spot in a crowd. This body part, which I've observed since childhood and never grown the slightest bit tired of, fascinates me. Exposed one moment, hidden the next, it forces you to stay alert for something that's really worth the effort. The photographer has to avoid blinking at the same time as his subject and capture the moment when the eye closes like a teasing oyster. I've come to believe that this work requires a special intuition, like an insect collector's, that there's not much difference between the flutter of a wing and the batting of an eyelash.

I count myself among the small percentage of people who care deeply about their work, and in that sense, I think I'm lucky. But don't get me wrong: our job does have its downsides. All kinds of people come through the studio, most of them desperate. The eyelids that end up here are almost all horrible, and they make you feel sorry, if not sick. It's no coincidence that their

owners want surgery. After two months of recovery,
when the patients, already transformed, come back for
the second session, we breathe a sigh of relief. While
few improve a hundred percent, the face—its expres-
sions, its permanent look—is completely changed: the
eyes seem better balanced. But if you look closely, especially when you've seen thousands of faces amended
by the same hand, you discover something atrocious:
somehow, they all look the same. As if Dr. Ruellan had
imprinted a distinctive mark on each patient, a faint
but unmistakable stamp.

Despite its pleasures, this profession, like any other,
eventually leads to indifference. I only recall a few
really memorable cases passing through our establish-
ment. When it happened, I would go to my father,
who was preparing the film in the back room, and
ask him to let me click the shutter. He always agreed,
though without understanding the cause of my sudden interest. One of these discoveries took place less
than a year ago, in November. During the winter, our
studio, on the ground floor of an old factory, becomes
unbearably damp; I'd rather be outside in bad weather
than stay in that cave, dark and frigid by necessity. My
father wasn't there that day, and I, freezing to death by
the door, amused myself with the rain's indecision and
cursed the client, who was more than fifteen minutes
late. When her figure finally appeared on the other side
of the gate, I was surprised she was so young, twenty

at most. A black waterproof hat covered her head, leaving the raindrops to slide down her long hair. Her left eyelid was a fraction of an inch lower than her right. Both eyes had a dreamy look, but the left was abnormally sensual, and seemed heavy. When I saw her I was overcome by an unusual sensation, a sort of pleasant inferiority I experience in the presence of excessively beautiful women.

With an exasperating lack of urgency, as if she couldn't care less about being late, she approached me to ask which floor the photographer was on. She must have taken me for the doorman.

"It's here," I told her. "You're standing at the entrance." I unlocked the door and, with a lofty gesture she couldn't have foreseen, I turned on all the lights, the way they do when a member of royalty appears in a ballroom. Once inside, she removed her hat. Her long black hair seemed like an extension of the rain. Like all the other patients, she explained that she'd made an appointment with Dr. Ruellan to fix her problem. *What problem?* I was about to ask. *You don't have one.* But I stopped myself. She was so young . . . I didn't want to upset her. I made a trivial comment instead:

"You're not from around here, are you?"

"I'm from Picardy," she replied timidly, avoiding eye contact, as patients usually do. But this time, I didn't appreciate the evasiveness; this time, it drove me crazy. I would have given anything to stare at that eyelid, which was somehow both heavy and fragile, all afternoon, and twice that to get those eyes to look back into mine.

"Do you like Paris?" I asked, feigning a distracted tone.

"Yes, but I can't stay long. I really came just for the operation."

"Paris will entice you, that's for sure. When you least expect it, you'll come here to live."

The girl smiled, lowering her head.

"I don't think so. I'd like to get back to Pontoise as soon as possible, I don't want to lose a whole year of credits for this."

The idea that this woman lived in another city was enough to make me miserable. I became moody. Suddenly, rudely perhaps, I interrupted our conversation to go get some film.

"Sit here," I said to her hurriedly when I got back. In all my professional life, I'd never been so unfriendly. The girl sat down on the bench and pushed back her hair to show her face.

"I don't know if you know this," I said, faking sympathy, "but the results are never perfect. This eye will never be the same as the other. Did the doctor explain that to you?"

She nodded.

"But he also told me that the two eyelids will be at the same level. For me, that's enough."

I thought about showing her a series of photos of

unsuccessful surgeries to try to discourage her. I could tell her that, no matter what, she'd end up with the unmistakable mark of Dr. Ruellan's patients, that mutant tribe. But I didn't have the courage. Without another word, I arranged the white backdrop behind her head and pointed the light toward her eyes. Instead of the usual three shots, I clicked the shutter fifteen times, and I would have gone on until nightfall if my father hadn't arrived.

Hearing the key turn in the lock, I switched off the studio lights. The young woman stood and went to the counter to sign the check, where I read her name in her schoolgirl's handwriting.

"Wish me luck," she said. "I'll see you in two months."

I can't describe the depression I fell into that night. I developed the photos immediately. I put the most conventional ones in an envelope with the hospital seal and kept the one I liked best in my desk drawer: a frontal portrait, dreamy and obscene.

My efforts to forget her were useless. I spent three months in terrified anticipation that she'd show up for the second series; I wanted to avoid her at all costs. Every Monday I checked my father's schedule so I'd know when to stay away. But she never came.

One early summer afternoon, walking by the river

in search of an interesting eyelid, I saw her again. The Seine was calm in those days; the stones reflected its dark green in gentle ripples. She was also staring at the river as she walked, so we almost bumped into each other. To my great surprise, her eyes were still the same. I greeted her politely and did everything possible to hide my joy, but after a few minutes, I couldn't hold back anymore:

"Did you change your mind?" I asked. "Did you decide not to go through with the operation?"

"Something came up and the doctor moved the date back to the end of the school year. I'm going into hospital tomorrow. Since I don't have any family in the city, I'll be there for three days."

"How are your studies going?"

"Last week I took my entry exam for the Sorbonne," she said, smiling. "I'd like to move to Paris."

She seemed happy. In her eyes, I saw that hopeful expression the patients often have on the eve of their surgeries, one that gives even the most deformed faces a candid look.

I invited her for an ice cream on the Île Saint-Louis. A jazz orchestra was playing nearby, and though we couldn't see the musicians from where we were, we could hear the notes from the banks as if they were coming up from the river. The sunlight tinted her eyelids orange. We walked for hours, sometimes in silence, other times talking about the things we saw, about the city and the future waiting for her here. If I'd brought the camera, I'd have some proof, not just of the ideal woman, but also of the happiest day of my life.

When it began to get dark, I walked her back to her hotel, a dump near Bonne Nouvelle. We spent the night together on a broken-down bed, in constant danger of tumbling onto the floor. With our clothes off, the twenty years' difference between us became more evident. I kissed her eyelids again and again, and when I got tired of that, I asked her to keep them open so I could enjoy that fraction of an inch of maddening sensuality. From the first embrace until the moment when, exhausted, I turned off the bedside lamp, I felt the need to convince her. Then, without shame or inhibition, I begged her not to have the operation, to stay with me, like this, just as she was in that moment. But she thought it was some romantic cliché, the sort of impassioned lie people tell in those situations.

We almost didn't sleep that night. If Dr. Ruellan, who demands absolute rest the night before a surgery, had known! She arrived at the pre-op wing of the hospital with dark circles under her eyes that made her seem older as well as more beautiful. I promised to stay with her until the last minute and to return as soon as she came round from the anesthesia. But it was impossible; the moment the nurse arrived to take her to the operating room, I escaped, slithering off to the elevator.

I left the hospital in pieces, as if retreating in defeat.

I thought about her so much the next day. I imagined her waking up alone, in that hostile room that smelled of disinfectant. I would have wanted to be there with her, if there weren't so much at stake: my memories, my image of those eyes, would vanish if I saw them after the operation, identical to those of all Dr. Ruellan's patients.

Some afternoons, especially during lean periods when the patients offer no satisfaction, I put her photograph on my desk and look at it for a few minutes. Seeing it there, I begin to suffocate, filled with infinite hatred toward our benefactor, as if in some way his scalpel had mutilated me, too. I haven't gone out with the camera since then. The banks of the Seine no longer hold any promise of mystery.

Through Shades

As in most of the apartments across the street, there's no light in your window now. It's been more than ten minutes since anyone walked by, and the wet asphalt is shining under the streetlights. I can't see you anymore, you flipped the switch exactly ten minutes ago, and the stillness makes me think you're not inside anymore. Though maybe I'm wrong, maybe I've misinterpreted everything and the whole night really happened another way, behind the two panes of glass that separate us.

Today, for the first time in months, I saw you go in with someone. You poured two glasses of whiskey and put some pretzels on the coffee table. She sat down on the living room sofa while you put the bottle back in the cabinet, as if announcing that this would be the only drink of a very short night. I've never heard your voice, but I'm sure that yesterday your words were dry and direct, almost cutting. In her eyes was the look of someone who'd made up her mind. Her legs had a sickly look to them, perhaps because of the gray tights she was wearing. Gray is an ugly color when you see it from far away. At first you seemed happy, almost euphoric. I don't know how many times you sat down next to her and got up again, indecisive. The host's smile on your lips looked as false as the leather of your armchairs. But your eyes were as sad as usual, perhaps a little more so. I felt sorry for you. In contrast with her puny legs, her breasts were large, luxuriant, exposed by her plunging neckline each time she leaned forward to take a pretzel. Her flimsy black dress was an invitation to strip her naked. I caught you letting your big sad eyes roam around in there several times. In that moment, I would have liked to be her, to be in her place, legs triumphantly opened, aware that you were mesmerized by her shoulders and neck, by her breasts in that low-cut top, which moved as leisurely and efficiently as the rudder of a ship on a steady course. You played along, but from time to time, you looked toward the street, sensing danger.

I never turned on the light. I went inside the apartment stealthily, hung my purse on the hook, and, in total darkness, made my way to the bedroom. The curtain was already drawn. I've left it that way since summer began and you moved into the building across the street. The chair is still there. It's the only one I use when I'm watching you, and for some strange reason, I think of it as lucky.

You barely drank anything. You let her put the last

of your drink in her glass and then vanished from view, reappearing in the kitchen, where the light falls more starkly on the sky-blue wall. You weren't smiling anymore. Instead, there was boredom on your face, the indecipherable scowl of a child on the verge of a tantrum. I saw you take ice cubes from the freezer, select another bag of pretzels, and something long you wrapped up in a napkin. But you didn't go back into the living room right away. You left the things you'd taken out beside the sink and lit a cigarette. In the living room window, she adjusted her gray tights and the neckline of her top, then sat still for a few minutes, waiting. Her glass was empty now, but she didn't take the initiative to stand up for the bottle; she didn't seem to know what to do. After a few drags, I saw you open the window and stub the cigarette out on the balcony. The wind didn't manage to erase the strained expression on your face. You closed the window again and stayed there a few minutes, leaning in the doorway. The shades were at half-mast, but I could still make out your silhouette easily. At that moment, a slight malaise came over me, a kind of dizziness. I looked up and saw you unbuckling your belt urgently, as if you couldn't breathe. For a few seconds I was able to observe your erect cock, before you began to move it back and forth in your hand, rapidly, forcefully. I was surprised by how dark it was, like the rings under your eyes. Down below, your boxers resting on your shoes. Above, your mouth, half-open. What would happen if she suddenly went looking for you in the kitchen? If she found you there, masturbating mid-date like someone who's been invited to a banquet and, just before sitting down at the table, ferociously raids the fridge?

She was still waiting there on the sofa, her legs together now. She looked like a little girl who had been punished but didn't know why. Meanwhile, I watched you from my room. I realized that I felt embarrassed, as if suddenly you were the intruder and I, the victim of your indiscretion. I started to feel wet between my thighs, a wetness as urgent as your movements. Without thinking, I opened the curtain a little so you might see me, a vain attempt to steal your last panting gasps. But the light was still off in my room, and your eyes, staring now at nothing, didn't catch my indiscreet gesture. Your hand sped up until, finally, you shot your load against the window. And without knowing why, I felt lighter then. Right away, without bothering to clean yourself up, you zipped your pants up. The expression on your face had changed. The glaring, bluish kitchen light went out, and you reappeared in the living room, where she received you expectantly. I tried to calm down, telling myself you hadn't seen me, regretting my recklessness and happy to watch you return to the living room, where she was waiting for you with her gray tights, her naïve little-girl face, and the little black dress she now wouldn't need to take off for the rest of the night.

Bonsai

Our bodies are like bonsai trees. Not one little innocent leaf can grow freely, without being viciously suppressed, so narrow is our ideal of appearance.

KHYENTSE NORBU

After I got married, I started taking walks in the Aoyama Botanical Garden every Sunday afternoon. It was a way of taking a break from work and domestic chores—if I stayed home on the weekend, Midori, my wife, would always end up asking me to fix something. After breakfast, I'd take a book and walk from our neighborhood to Shinjuku Avenue, where I'd enter the garden through the east gate. That way, I could walk by fountains, cross the lines of trees in the courtyard, and, if the sun was shining, sit down to read on a bench. On rainy days, I'd go to the café—almost always empty at that time—and settle down by a window to read. Going home, I'd leave the garden

21

through the back gate, where the guard would nod politely in recognition.

Though I went to the park every Sunday, it was years before I entered the greenhouse. As a little boy, I'd learned to enjoy gardens and forests, but I'd never been interested in individual plants. To me, a garden was an architectural and green space where you could go alone, but only if you had something to read or amuse yourself with, and where you could even take clients to close a good deal. When I was young, I'd gone to that same garden with a girl from school and, later on, a college girlfriend, but neither of them had thought to visit the greenhouse, either. I admit that the building wasn't exactly enticing: it looked more like a chicken coop or storehouse than an enclosed garden. I imagined it to be an oppressive place, maddening like Tsukiji Market, though smaller and filled with unknown plants that had unpronounceable names.

One afternoon, however, I suddenly took an interest in the greenhouse. I remember it was the Thursday of a long weekend. We had decided not to go out of town, and in the air there was a Sunday kind of atmosphere. Maybe that's why I had the urge to take a walk among the trees. It wasn't really the most suitable day for a stroll: as I was leaving, my wife pointed out that it had started to rain. I picked up my book and a large umbrella and got ready to leave the apartment. But just when I was about to pull the gate to our building shut,

Midori appeared smiling on the stairs, with her rain-coat on, and announced that she was coming with me.

We hadn't gone for a walk together in that garden since before we married. After so many years, Aoyama had turned into a space reserved for me, one of those places you gradually make your own and that constitute a kind of refuge, an island cut off from contact with other people. I won't deny that the idea of Midori joining me on Sundays made me feel slightly uneasy. Even so, I didn't object. When I decided to get married I resolved to share everything with her, and I liked to make it known that there were no secrets between us.

We entered the garden through the east gate, as I always did, and waved to the guard, who seemed pleased to see me with a companion. He must have wondered about my domestic situation, since he'd never seen me with anyone else. Besides, Midori and I were the perfect image of a happy couple; we looked made for each other—or so we'd been told ad nauseum since our wedding day, so often that we'd ended up believing it. Midori really likes the rain and was in high spirits that day. I remember her under the umbrella, waving her hands about as she spoke of her teenage years in Aoyama. Although we hadn't known each other then, Midori and I had both grown up in that neighborhood, and both felt a special fondness for it.

"Back then, I used to come to this park as often as

you do," she said, as if trying to recover a certain authority. "Isn't it strange that we never saw each other?"

My wife went around the park several times, inspecting everything, like a property owner returned from a long absence to take stock of the ravages of time. Meanwhile, I held the umbrella that covered us both. When it seemed like she'd never tire of walking around, she stopped suddenly, as if she'd remembered something.

"Of course!" she said, her eyes wide. "The greenhouse!" And she slipped out from beneath the umbrella and ran off toward the ancient building. With my feet sinking slightly into the wet ground, I watched her head for the door without moving from my spot.

But the greenhouse was closed, and Midori was as disappointed as she had been enthusiastic before.

"I really would have liked to see the old man again," she exclaimed.

I didn't know whom she was talking about, so I asked her.

"There was a gardener here who I used to sit and talk with. He'd tell me all sorts of things! Nobody else liked to talk to him. My classmates all said he gave them nervous stomachs, like a bad omen. But I was fond of him, and he never did anything to upset me."

"They really said that?" I asked, genuinely interested. "What did he talk to you about?"

"I can't really remember, to be honest; about plants, I think."

"How can plants cause a nervous stomach unless you're eating them or making them into tea?" I asked.

We laughed and started talking about something else. The rest of the afternoon in the Aoyama garden went by as peacefully as it began. Midori and I went home early and gave in to our lust until we fell asleep. On Monday, as I stared attentively at the rug in my office, I found myself thinking about the gardener. I was very familiar with the guard who greeted me from the booth at the entrance, I also knew the guy who pruned the bushes in the spring and planted flowers around the fountains, but in all my years of going there, I'd never seen Midori's gardener. If this man were still there, my wife had the upper hand when it came to who had ownership of the garden.

The next Sunday, I couldn't resist heading straight to the greenhouse, but I saw no one. I went over to the booth and asked the guard about the old man.

"He doesn't come on Sundays," he said. "Why do you want to see him?" In his face, I thought I noticed some concern.

"My wife knows him and asked me to say hello," I lied.

"He's hardly ever here anymore, he's too old to still be working, but if you come around on a Saturday, with a little luck, you'll find him."

So I went another week without meeting the gardener.

On Saturdays, Midori usually spent the whole afternoon at the salon. Like the walk in Aoyama for me, her cosmetic routine was a space she reserved for herself, and just the idea of seeing me pass by the window would have made her hair stand on end. I, on the other hand, rarely knew what to do with myself at those times. Sometimes I'd read the newspaper a second time or watch a game on TV. I remember it was raining that Saturday, a dirty rain like melted hail. Unlike my wife, I hated the rain. Nevertheless, as soon as Midori left the apartment, I put on my raincoat and set off for Aoyama. It was unlikely that the gardener would be there on an afternoon like that at his age, but as soon as I got to the greenhouse, I saw him on his knees, wearing a gray uniform and working the soil in a flowerpot. I approached slowly and respectfully.

"Well, look who it is!" the old man exclaimed. "What brings you here on a Saturday, Mr. Okada?" His question unnerved me. I was ashamed to say I had come by just to see him, so I evaded his question by changing the subject.

"How did you know I only come on Sundays?" I asked.

"A gardener knows all the worms in his territory, even the ones who only show up every once in a while."

I smiled. Although his joke seemed a little daring, I felt no trace of the nervous stomach Midori had mentioned. On the contrary, the old man seemed pleasant, and I felt like spending some time with him.

And so I stayed in the greenhouse, watching him

work. Unlike the other garden employees, he didn't wear gloves; he'd rake the earth with a tiny trowel and pull up the weeds with his wrinkled fingers. Now, almost a year later, just the memory of those blackened nails is enough to make me sad, but at the time his hands seemed curious, as if they belonged to a goblin or some character in a story.

The gardener returned to his work in silence. So as not to bother him, I took a little tour of the greenhouse, pretending to be interested in the names of the different species they stored there, but it wasn't long before I came back. When he saw me, the old man lifted his head and cast me a watery look. His black eyes seemed to be floating in their large sockets. As the elderly often do, he had a somewhat childlike expression, like someone who still allows the world to surprise him.

"Do you like plants, Mr. Okada?" he asked in a serious voice.

"To be honest, they've never interested me," I replied.

"I should have known. You're one of the ones who just come here to walk in the park, right? If you showed up one Sunday and instead of pine trees there was a row of cypresses, it would all be the same to you, or maybe you wouldn't even notice."

"You're probably right," I admitted. "As long as there isn't much of a difference between a pine and a cypress." (The truth was I had no idea what a cypress tree looked like.)

The old man looked at me without saying a word. Perhaps to a fanatical gardener what I'd just said could be interpreted as an insult, but there was no trace of offense in his face or his dark, watery eyes.

"I don't blame you," he said at last. "You have to really know plants to love them, and you also have to know them to hate them."

"Hate them?" I asked.

"Plants are living beings, Mr. Okada, and your relationship with them is like a relationship with any living being. Are you not interested in animals, either?"

I recalled a dog I had owned in high school. After those first few glorious weeks my sister and I spent playing with him, he ended up abandoned in the kitchen. I don't even remember how he disappeared from the house.

"The truth is . . ." I started to speak.

"Well, you may not realize it, but plants are worse than animals. If you don't take care of them, they die. Let's face it: it's endless blackmail. Plant one and you'll see. As soon as the first leaf appears, you'll have to keep watering it; when it gets too big, you'll have to repot it, and maybe later on it'll catch some disease. Don't be fooled, Mr. Okada: plants are a nuisance."

I looked around. In the greenhouse, all the plants looked perfectly tended and shiny. Everything seemed to be in its rightful place: the plants that needed light were in the sun, and the ones that needed shade were in the darker part at the back of the shed. The gardener seemed to carry out his work perfectly.

"If they annoy you so much," I asked, "why do you still bother taking care of them?"

"Let's say it's a commitment," he answered tersely. "Some of us have a sense of duty, though not everyone knows what that is. When I took the job in the greenhouse, I signed on to care for these plants, and that's what I'm going to do, until I can't anymore."

The next day I didn't leave the house. Since I'd been there on Saturday afternoon, I didn't go back to Aoyama. I stayed in to humor my wife, who, predictably, charged me with dozens of tasks, like fixing the door to the kitchen (the lock didn't work and had to be changed) and installing a new bathroom shelf (her makeup no longer fit in the cabinet). Then we watched TV, and even though Midori made several attempts, that night we didn't give in to lust. I didn't mention my greenhouse visit, either.

That's how I started going to Aoyama on Saturday afternoons instead of on Sundays. I didn't go in through the east gate anymore, the way I had for years, but instead went straight to the entrance nearest the greenhouse. And I no longer walked around among the trees or sat down to read on a bench. When he saw me arrive, the old man didn't look surprised anymore, but instead welcomed me with a smile of recognition. Also, as time passed, he spoke to me less and less. He would

generally limit himself to comments about whichever
plant he was pruning. It reminded me a little of the
atmosphere established between two people who are
used to sharing an office. Only I wasn't working with
the gardener, just sitting near him, lighting one cigarette after another as I watched him. Little by little, I
became familiar with his work, but also with the plants.
A few of them began to stand out to me more than others. When I grew tired, I'd say goodbye and leave the
greenhouse for the café across the way. It might seem
stupid, but that's how I spent my Saturdays, and to me,
it all felt like a real adventure. I don't know if it was
watching the gardener work, looking at the plants, or
the furtiveness of it all, since I still hadn't said anything
to Midori. And, as often happens, I had to do a kind of
balancing act to preserve the secrecy. On Sundays, for
example, I'd take some book from my study and leave
the house as if I were going to walk in the garden, but I
actually went to the Jenjiko café a few blocks away from
our building. That's how, almost without realizing, I let
a whole month go by and still hadn't broached the subject with Midori. *After all*, I told myself, *she was the one
who told you about him, and you only went to the greenhouse because of all her memories. Why keep it a secret?* It
was as if I were stealing something from her, something
I refused give back. But instead of shame, this theft
brought me a pleasure I had no desire to relinquish,
and just as a thief clings to his loot, absurd as it might

seem, I refused to bring up the topic with my wife. But this pleasure wasn't going to last long, either.

As I said, the plants were beginning to seem more interesting, or at least not as boring as before. It's not that I had become a botany fanatic, but suddenly they'd taken on a kind of personality. In short, they were no longer objects, but living beings. One day, for instance, I noticed that the gardener never paid any attention to the cacti. There they were, forgotten in their dry, coppery earth. Some erect like sentinels, others curled up at ground level, in the guarded stance of a hedgehog. I went over to their planter and observed them for a few minutes. There seemed to be no movement in them, aside from that stiff and somewhat defensive attitude. The many tiny thorns on their greenish skin made me think of my own face when I went more than two days without shaving. According to my wife, I have too much hair to be Japanese. But, beyond the beard, I felt that the cacti and I had something in common (there was a reason I found them so endearing, though I also felt a little sorry for them). They were so different from the other plants, the expansive ferns or the palms. The more I looked at them, the more I understood them. They must have felt lonely in that big greenhouse, with no chance of communicating even among one another. The cacti were the outsiders of the greenhouse; that, along with their consequential defensiveness, was their only shared trait. *If I'd been born a plant*, I admitted to myself, *I could only have belonged to that species.*

The question was inevitable and came swiftly: If I was of the Cactaceae family, what was Midori? The woman I had chosen to share my life with was clearly no cactus. Nothing about them reminded me of her. It's true that Midori was also fragile, but in another way; she wasn't on the defense, brandishing spines in every direction. No, she had to be something else, something much gentler but also not completely incompatible. I spent Saturday afternoon examining every species in the greenhouse but didn't succeed in finding the one that resembled Midori.

As the days passed, my place in the cactus family became more and more evident. At the office, I sat straight and tall, anticipating the moment when the door would open to let in bad news. Every time the phone rang, I felt a new spine push through my skin.

In reality, this was nothing new. Like my school-mates had before, my colleagues often joked about my stark temperament, but they'd never taken it too seriously. Now, however, everything seemed like a logical consequence of my condition. It was so simple: I was a cactus; they were not. Every once in a while, in an elevator or some hallway, I just might recognize another cactus. Then we'd have no choice but to greet each other, avoiding each other's eyes.

I felt liberated. I stopped worrying about things that, before, had bothered me or made me anxious, like not being able to dance. Midori, who danced with

exceptional sensuality, always scolded me for my stiff-
ness. "It is what it is," I could now respond cynically.
"You chose to marry a cactus." Around that time, I
also stopped smiling hypocritically at the colleagues I
ran into in the office lunchroom, something I'd been
doing for years. It wasn't a lack of friendliness, just simply being consistent with my nature. Surprisingly, no
one took it badly. In fact, my colleagues remarked that
lately I seemed "in good shape," even "more natural."

There were also some changes at home. When I had
nothing to say, I didn't speak. From then on, I refused
to maintain pretend conversations with Midori about
her pedicure, her new dress, or whatever had happened
to her friend Shimamoto on vacation; most of all, I
stopped feeling guilty for not telling her about my
friendship with the gardener. That didn't mean I loved
her less; on the contrary, the more I became myself, the
better I could relate to the world. But Midori didn't
take it the same way. Asserting myself as a cactus made
her exaggerate all her reactions. She was always asking me where I'd spent the afternoon, and as if that
weren't enough, her libido became very persistent. In
the mornings before work or at night before we went
to sleep, Midori felt the urge to make love, which, of
course, went against my cactus nature.

One night, after a nightmare I couldn't remember,
I was startled awake. The almost-full moon streamed
through the shoji, painting the room a bluish light.

Midori's body was practically on top of mine, deeply asleep and breathing calmly. Her legs and arms were wrapped around mine like branches of ivy or honeysuckle. And that's how I knew that my wife was a climbing vine, soft and shiny. *That's why she likes rain so much*, I thought, *while I can't stand it.* I lay there thinking about Midori for several minutes, about her quiet way of infiltrating any space and taking possession of my life. The more I thought about it, the further away sleep felt. Luckily, I remembered my schedule for the next day: I had an important meeting at 9 a.m. I had to try to sleep.

I had a hard time waking up that morning and took a longer shower than usual. All through breakfast, my wife was silent. She seemed upset about something.

"Are you feeling OK?" I asked the question affectionately but avoided touching her.

"Yes, don't worry. It's just the dream I had last night."

"What dream?" I blurted out, noting anxiety in my voice.

Midori took a deep breath.

"I dreamed we had a baby, a beautiful little baby boy. We've never talked about that," she explained, looking at me inquisitively, as if trying to decipher my thoughts. I shivered.

I looked at my watch in alarm: I was fifteen minutes late.

"We'll talk tonight. I promise."

Midori and I had been married for eight years. Almost all our couple friends had children. When they asked us what we did to look so happy, we'd always say the secret was not having them. It was strange that Midori had brought this up just after I'd discovered her true identity.

The meeting with our client that morning was a total disaster; I couldn't concentrate on the conversation for even a minute, much less convince him to sign a contract. I decided to take the afternoon off and go to Aoyama. As soon as I reached the greenhouse, I started looking for a climbing vine to confirm my discovery. As I searched, I almost tripped over the gardener, who was scratching at the earth in a potted plant like a kitten. He seemed surprised to see me.

"Shouldn't you be working, Mr. Okada?" he asked, moving over to a bush he began to prune with both hands.

"I left early today," I said, and almost immediately I added: "What do you think about vines?"

The gardener put down the pruning shears and looked at me, surprised.

"The strength of a plant like that," he said, "is rooted in its unwavering willpower. They're capable of climbing from the ground to the top of a tower. Their advantage is, they survive no matter where you put them, they can adapt to any climate."

There was a strange inflection in the gardener's voice, as if he were about to announce some bad news. For a moment, I thought he already knew everything.

"And those plants," I asked, feeling even more uneasy, "do they have a special breeding period?"

The old man took some time before answering.

"It depends, some of them do it every month, others every week. Why do you think they grow so fast?"

"And cacti?" I asked.

"Cacti are another thing entirely. Some of them reproduce only once in a lifetime, and generally right before they die." As he said this, he stood and put the shears back in their pouch. "Come with me," he said, "I'm going to show you something."

The gardener led me to the pot that contained a few cacti I'd seen several times, but one of them now had a red flower at its tip.

"This one is a special case. It can live to be eighty years old and reproduces every twenty. But that's not what I wanted to show you," he said, "this is."

Beside the pot of cacti, an inch off the floor, I noticed a gray rectangular container that hadn't been there before. The container held a miniature reproduction of the Aoyama garden. There was the café, the rectangular fountains, the greenhouse, and also the rows of pines and cherry trees.

"Are they real?" I asked, surprised. And as I said this, I realized we were whispering, like two people sharing a secret.

The gardener's only reply was to shake his head, but in such an ambiguous way that I didn't know if he meant yes or no.

Bonsai have always prompted a kind of fear in me, or at least a puzzling discomfort. I hadn't seen any for a long time, and coming across so many of them at once made me feel almost physically unwell. The old man must have noticed and said:

"I feel the same way. They're an aberration."

I was surprised to hear it from the mouth of a gardener, but at the same time, that word corresponded so closely to what I was feeling.

"Why are they here?" I asked irritably, my voice rising slightly. "Why did you bring me over to see this?"

"I've been cultivating them for many years. I've pruned each one of their leaves, seen them dry up and fall into the earth in the pot, simulating the death rattle of real trees but without making any kind of noise. Take a good look, Mr. Okada," he insisted while I examined the miniature bark as if some answer were hidden within. "I think you've learned to look closely enough at plants to realize: these aren't plants, and they're not trees, either. Trees are the most expansive beings on earth, a bonsai, on the other hand, is a contraction. Whether they come from a leafy tree or a fruit tree, bonsais are just that, bonsais: trees that betray their true nature."

I walked home in the rain. Since I didn't have an umbrella, my clothes were dripping when I arrived. The whole way, I was thinking about the climbing vine and the cactus. A cactus would suffer in a rainy climate like this, but a vine would be happy there. I loved Midori, but allowing her to encroach on me was contrary to my nature. I also thought about how betrayed and unhappy a vine would feel if unable to reproduce.

I went inside and took a hot shower. Midori was busy with some galley proofs she had to send to print that same night, so, fortunately, we didn't discuss reproduction.

Saturday I went to Aoyama, but the old man wasn't in the greenhouse. I asked the guard where he was, but he didn't have any explanation. Apparently, they were used to the old man disappearing for a few days. I waited in the café to see if he'd suddenly show up, but after a while I realized it was useless.

When I got home, Midori was there. She'd just returned from the salon. Like every Saturday, her hair was very smooth, almost the way the water made it look when she'd just gotten out of the shower.

"Why are you looking at me like that?" she asked.

"Like what?" I answered. "What did you do to your hair?"

"The same thing as always," she said, annoyed.

This was true: her hair was the same as ever, and so were her nails. There was nothing new, but I still couldn't help but find her different, as if instead of returning Midori to me, the people at the salon had sent her double.

"You're right, it's the same," I said to end the discussion. I was very hungry and didn't want to run the risk of delaying dinner with an absurd argument. Besides, what could I say—that today she looked like a replica of herself? We ate dinner in silence while Rossini's *La gazza ladra* played on the radio. Then I realized: I was sitting in front of a perfect bonsai. The bonsai was a climbing vine.

I thought the feeling would pass, but that night, before going to sleep, I noticed the contraction of those dwarf trees in her worried face again. When Midori tried to stretch her branches around my body, I could only reject her. Every night that week was the same, and a profound disquiet was growing in me.

One night my wife couldn't stand it anymore and got angry:

"What's the matter with you? For days now you've been looking at me like I were an alien!"

She was right, but what explanation could I give her? Even I didn't know what to think.

I got up from bed and went out onto the balcony to smoke a cigarette. The moon was waning, and the sight of it made me profoundly sad. Where was Midori, my wife, the woman with whom I'd decided to share my life? She was there—there was no doubt about it—but why couldn't I see her the way I had before? Midori was there in the room, but she had turned into a climbing vine, just as I had turned into a cactus. But hadn't we always been like that? How could I know for sure? I felt alone in the world, trapped in a perspective I'd never escape. At a distance, in the bedroom, I heard Midori sobbing—expansively, the way she did everything—and her cry penetrated the deepest corners of my consciousness. I reproached myself for my attitude: if I'd just told her about my greenhouse visits and my relationship with the old man, things wouldn't have taken on such a terrifying dimension. If she had gone with me that first Saturday afternoon, we could have lived the adventure together. We'd be sharing a story now, not living with this stupid point of view between us like soundproof glass. I decided not to return to the greenhouse.

A few months later, Midori and I separated.

It was a year before I was able to go back to the garden. Since that day when the gardener wasn't there to meet me, I hadn't returned to take walks in that park. What could have happened to the old man? I couldn't help but associate him with my divorce and the sadness that, ever since then, I felt in my deepest roots, a feeling not at all like an upset stomach. I realized that in some way I blamed him, and I felt the need to tell him so. So I looked for him everywhere, but I never found him.

Finally I asked the guard at the booth about him, and he looked as surprised as someone seeing an apparition.

"Mr. Murakami is in the hospital; he's very ill," the guard explained, lowering his eyes respectfully.

It was the first time I'd heard the gardener's name. I thought of the old man, helpless and dying in the hospital, anxious over the fate of his plants. I thought of the ten years that had passed since Midori and I moved from the Aoyama neighborhood to Jenjiko, to our married couple's apartment. I thought of my life with a climbing vine and how quickly it came to an end. Most of all, I remembered the longevity of the cactus: eighty years or more in dry, coppery earth.

The Other Side
of the Dock

for Aimee

*Friendship is an imperceptible
drama, a series of subtle insults.*

EMIL CIORAN

The Trouble With Being Born

Over the years I've heard all sorts of opinions on True
Solitude. It's one of those topics that often come up at
family dinners, the kind that, like current events and
questions of morality, discourage sincere expression
since they tend to lead to entanglements in the inflated
fibroids of misunderstanding. Some people, especially
those leaning toward old age, describe True Solitude
as a sturdy web we build over the years, but others say
it's a rare, whimsical space with quite arbitrary laws of
access. When my better judgment is drowned out by

the chatter—by so many pairs of eyeglasses, the sipping of tea, aunts with makeup caked on their faces, and some child stretching a sticky hand toward the cookies on a tray—I defend that definition, because I remember, not without a certain nostalgia, seeking out that paradise when I was fifteen. According to me, the only inhabitant of True Solitude would be a girl who, back then, was embarrassed by her pointy new breasts, which looked like they belonged to a skinny animal; by the body too big for her dresses and too slight for her bathing suit. Whenever I think about that, I can't help but want to smile discreetly, lowering my head a little so the family doesn't see, but it's impossible, because while Clara swats at the little boy's handful of sweets, I once again see that summer in Santa Helena, the fishermen's island where she and Toño decided to invent a house they called the House of the Orange Trees, and the memory immediately freezes my smile.

In that era, my solitude wasn't True but oppressive and mediocre, suffused with snide laughter in a sordid high school in Mexico City. I was the niece, and Clara, my mother's younger sister. To set her apart from the others, who wore high heels even at home and spent whole mornings at the salon, I didn't call her "aunt." She was an energetic twenty-eight-year-old PE teacher in an alternative primary school, and she had a convertible Volkswagen no one believed could make it to the coast. She also had a boyfriend my grandmother detested—that alone was enough to endear Toño to me. By then, my fights with my parents had begun to take on more lifelike dimensions, so I hardly had to convince them to let me go off to that half-deserted island, where the two of them had come by the House of the Orange Trees at an absurdly low price.

When they came for me, the car was packed with several suitcases, a cooler, newly framed paintings, and the toolbox they'd need to get the house back into working order.

"Put whatever you want in the back," they said, pointing to a trunk that was crammed to the top. I tried to take as little as possible so nothing would distract me from my search.

After several hours of driving, when the road had become a scale model crowded with plants, sea air, and *guacamayas*, we left the car for the motorboat that would drop us off at the dock. We arrived late in the afternoon, and to my delight, everything, except a few palm trees whipped by the wind, was still. As soon as we landed, I realized that Clara had fooled the family: there were no orange trees, and the gorgeous English-style house was barely the memory of a ruin, the roof a layer of wood on the verge of collapsing.

"It's almost perfect, the planks are going to hold up really well. As long as it doesn't rain, it'll be ready in no time," she said with her characteristic enthusiasm, placing one hand on my head as if to dissolve all my worries. From the other side, Toño embraced her, nuzzling up against her neck with his mustache. But the fragility of the roof hadn't had any effect on my joy. I was sure that if I were ever going to access True Solitude, it could only happen here.

Half the island was a fishing village, and the other half, where we spent that entire summer, an empty beach with a few homes, most of them enormous and uninhabited. This was where the house was, and Toño and Clara intended to fix it up in two weeks, then enjoy the last seven days of their vacation.

The first week in Santa Helena was one long siesta in the sun. I thought it would all be so easy once I was there, just a matter of waiting, of concentrating on an endless strip of sand until paradise came on its own and surrounded me with its silence. The heat was unerring, day and night, and rain was about as likely as trees springing up from the sand. Clara and Uncle Toño—I liked to call him that, especially in front of Grandma—spent mornings and afternoons repairing the roof of the house. Far away, lying on the sand but always in my clothes, since I couldn't stand the idea of some neighbor seeing me in a bathing suit, I'd listen to the background noise of their hammerings and brief remarks, try to recognize things in the shapes of the clouds, and fall asleep thinking that even if I didn't realize it, I was entering paradise.

When night began to fall, when the light of the

sun was a faint pill of vitamin C dissolving over the water, the two would go into the house to shower and smear creams on their dry, tanned skin. Then came the nightly dinner party: Clara would light candles all over the house and bring in a tray of canned seafood she'd bought in Mexico, because their work on the roof and my fear of seeing any people kept us from going into the village for food. But the candlelight, our hunger, and the quiet made those moments, tin cans and all, modest explosions of harmony.

The few boats that came to Santa Helena would leave from the coast at 7 a.m. and return in the late afternoon. Most of the time, the only passengers were those who came with baskets of fruit and bread to sell in the village. Every day they passed by the house, a commotion of shouting and portable radios that lasted just a few minutes. Then the beach returned to its usual state: the same strip of sand cut off from everything, where there was no room for high school, the trouble of talking to people my own age—especially boys—or my parents' outrageous insults. Only occasionally would small groups of tourists show up on the island, probably on the advice of some overzealous tour guide who'd describe the abandoned homes and the fruit peels adorning the entrance to town like some picturesque landscape. Those days it was better to stay inside, far from awkward stares and affected little smiles—gringos will strike up a conversation with anyone who

lets them. But in the house, I surrendered to the temp-
tation of standing in front of the mirror, examining the
ravages of my acne or my budding breasts, which were
ugly and sometimes sore. Almost immediately, I would
recall the remarks at school, my uncontrollable blush-
ing in front of anyone of the opposite sex, and little by
little, the door to True Solitude would melt away.

Very early, almost every morning, I'd wait for the
boat on the dock, consulting the vague smell of gas-
oline and shellfish to figure out what kind of day it
would be. Looking at the sea for too long made me
feel sick, I'd inevitably think of biology class, of the
teacher's amphibious hands explaining the cycle of life,
of all those fish reproducing so close to me, in a luke-
warm, salty broth. Did Clara and Toño also intend to
reproduce at some point? Some nights I found them
kissing at the front door, from where you could see the
moon drowning in the water. But I didn't think they
would go that far—and if and when they did, I would
stop calling Clara's boyfriend "uncle." The only way to
save myself, to avoid becoming like them, was to concentrate on the search for my paradise: *I need to forget
about everything*, I'd say to myself, *leave behind all memories of the city in the landscape of this island*. But True
Solitude came concealed in a boat and spent several
days on our beach before making itself known to me.

Michelle arrived in Santa Helena on one of those
noisy crossings, along with fishermen and fruit baskets.

I saw her out on the sea long before the boat docked, and immediately realized that my project would have complications. She didn't look like someone who'd come to lie in the sun; she looked like a girl my age, maybe the bitchy blonde at some high school showing up on the island in a tight little dress, and that wasn't the worst part: next to her bare feet, there was an enormous suitcase that seemed as definitive as an anchor. Michelle let everyone take their goods off the boat, let the women take their portable radios out from among the fruit and the men begin pounding octopus against the planks, before placing ten red nails on the swollen wood rail of our dock.

Her arrogant blue eyes surveyed the landscape, then the house, the roof that Clara and Toño were hammering, the broken-down *palapa*, the remains of a chair in the sand, a mangy chicken that must have escaped from the village and was now roaming around among fruit peels. Then, with the same indifference, she looked at me, at the little animals on the towel I was carrying over my shoulder. Without a word, without even a gesture, she dragged her suitcase off toward one of the huge houses looming over the cliff, and since she stayed away for the rest of the day, by the time a few hours had passed, I felt almost able to act as if no one had arrived. What worried me was that there might be other people in her house. I didn't think the newcomer was the type to spend her vacations alone, and the idea of being surrounded by her brothers or cousins was frankly unbearable. It alarmed me to think that, even if they weren't here yet, the island might soon be filled with bikini-clad girls playing volleyball on the sand. Back at the house, I didn't ask any questions: denying Michelle's arrival was a silent ritual to block any possibility of closeness.

One night, while I was trying as hard as I could to renew my search at the far end of the living room, Clara came into the dining room with a newly unpacked red apron and a wooden tray filled with shells.

"They're oysters," she said. "I bought them in town this morning, we went for a walk while you were down at the dock. By the way, did you see anyone on the beach?"

"Nobody," I answered, trying to act surprised, but Clara went on:

"In town, I heard Ms. Neuville's daughter has come over from France—her name is Michelle, or something like that. The mother is very sick, so she lives in that house on the cliff for most of the year. I met her when I came to make the arrangements for our place."

I said nothing else and focused on chasing the elusive slime inside its shell with my fork. Soon the wind began to pick up over the palm fronds, and the conversation returned to the usual topic:

"Just a little more hammering," said Toño, "and then we'll be doing the same thing you are—looking up at the sky from a towel."

The calm didn't last long. Amid gusts of wind, I heard a distinctly urgent knocking on the window, but I said nothing. The knocking persisted, getting louder and louder until even Clara and Toño noticed it from within their conversation and decided to go and look outside. It seems my intuition was well founded: just speaking of the intruder had invoked her. On the other side of the window, Michelle's hair was like the top of a *palapa*, palm fronds shaken by the wind. Clara opened the front door and invited her in for dinner with her alternative-school teacher's voice.

"We're eating oysters, would you like some?"

The girl answered in very correct Spanish, colored with the slightest nasal tone.

"No, thanks so much. I actually came over to ask a favor."

Clara sat down again, the back of the chair between her legs, and made a show of paying special attention.

"Of course, ask away."

Another proactive approach that seemed to go unnoticed by the French girl, whose blue eyes, at that moment, were focused on me with unmistakable annoyance, surely the same I'd felt upon seeing her in the house. Clara repeated the invitation.

"I'd like to climb up on your roof," said Michelle.

This time no teacherly reply could hide our confusion.

"Are you sure?" asked Toño, coming to the rescue. "I don't think that would be much fun."

"I'm not trying to have fun," she said, almost offended. "Your roof is the only place on this island where someone's making an effort to fix all the decay."

There was a silent exchange of glances in which Toño and Clara consulted each other as if I weren't there; after coming to a number of understandings, they gave Michelle permission to go up on the roof for a while on the condition that I go with her.

I promised myself I'd be unfriendly; I promised myself I wouldn't say a word unless I was asked a question. I climbed up first, and as soon as I was on the roof, I pulled up the ladder so the French girl had to take twice as long climbing the wall. She never asked for my help or for me to lower the ladder. When she finally sat down on the edge of the roof, she took two cigarettes from her skirt pocket.

"Do you smoke?" she said, aggressively friendly.

I shook my head no.

"Why?" she asked, the smile still on her face.

"I want to avoid lung cancer."

Michelle granted me a few minutes of silence before resuming the attack.

"What a personality! I bet you don't have many friends."

Then it was my turn to stay quiet for a while.

"Do you have a lot?" I asked.

"Yes, and I have a boyfriend, too. His name is Philippe. I'll introduce you when he gets here."

My stomach knotted up around my belly button. I didn't want to meet anyone, especially not another surly French person, and if either of them started coming down to the beach, the objective of my summer would be doomed to resounding failure. But I didn't ask any questions, just let Michelle talk while she finished off her second cigarette. Afterward, I put the ladder back in place and announced that it was time for us to go back to our houses.

I didn't see her again for several days. But I had to try hard to renew my search for True Solitude; Michelle's voice was the kind that reverberates in your head. Without realizing it, I started to ask myself questions: How old was she? How had she met Philippe? One night, while we were opening cans in the kitchen, I asked Clara if she'd been to the house where the French women lived.

"Is it pretty?"

"Yes, but it's too modern for my taste," she answered, looking proudly at our damp walls. "I prefer the House of the Orange Trees. Have you seen the girl again? No? The poor thing must barely go out, with her mother so sick."

"What does she have?" I asked, surprised. I had forgotten that detail.

"I'm not sure, something serious, lung cancer, I think."

I finished setting the table but couldn't eat anything during dinner. Before Clara and Toño went out to look at the moon as they did every night, I went to my room and stayed there for hours, trying to sleep, until I heard the knocking on the window.

"Can you come out for a second?" Michelle said from the other side of the glass.

I thought her boyfriend must have arrived on the evening boat, that she wanted to introduce him to me, so at first, I curled up under the covers and pretended to be sound asleep, but when I looked more carefully, I saw she was alone.

"Do you want to go up on the roof?" I asked.

"Yes, but I didn't ask permission."

"That's OK, it's almost finished," I said. "Besides, it's impossible to bother them when it's this late. At night, Toño and Clara can really be too much, you must know how it is."

We climbed up. The moon looked like a tangle of radiant clouds, and the sea was rougher than ever. When we sat, the planks let out a long groan that ended with a crack.

"Why did they bring you here?" Michelle asked, hugging her knees to her chest. Her red nails were ten mouths smiling on her bare feet.

"They didn't bring me. I came because I wanted to be alone."

"You never talk to anyone, not even at school?"

"I hate school. During recess, I stay in the classroom. Sometimes I take out a book to make sure no one bothers me."

"But nobody does, obviously," she said.

"How do you know?"

"It's the same everywhere, people realize that deep down you're dying to talk to them and you're playing hard to get. Just like you did with me the other night."

"That's not true," I answered, turning away.

"Your parents, though, they definitely want to talk, and they want you to talk back. That's just how it is: they realize you're not interested in them. Families only talk about whatever they're going through. Lucky for me, my mom barely talks at all."

"What does she talk about?" I asked.

"About nothing, death. And your family?"

"About True Solitude, but I don't think that's what they're going through. When is your boyfriend coming to visit?"

"Philippe? He's not coming. I just said that to impress you. And he's really not even my boyfriend anymore, he broke up with me when he found out I was going away for so long. He says in Mexico you catch rare diseases."

"Then you shouldn't have come."

The roof made another crack, so we decided to climb down right away; besides, it was getting late.

"I have to go home. My mother has insomnia almost every night, and she wants me to be with her," she said before adjusting the ladder. "I think she's afraid."

"And you're not?" I asked as I helped her down, almost regretting it.

"I am, but it's different. When your mom is afraid, it's like suddenly she can't feed you anymore, like this time she's really taken her breast out of your mouth. You know what I mean?"

Like hell, I thought, and stayed silent.

"Come over whenever you want," I said when we reached the door. I could tell she was sad and wanted to hug her but didn't dare.

Two days later, it was cloudy, so I didn't go out to the dock or the *palapa*. For the first time since we'd left for vacation, I didn't think about True Solitude at all.

In the afternoon, it started to rain. It was a rough drizzle, tossed around by the wind. Clara called out to Toño to show him the drops on the window.

"Don't worry," he said. "Our roof will hold up just fine."

"That's not what I'm worried about," she said. "All we have left in the kitchen is a box of Havana cookies, we need to go out and get food. If this turns into a storm, it could last all week."

"I can't stand those cookies," Toño said.

I thought it would be a good time to look for Michelle, but before I could prepare for the expedition, they left without saying goodbye. I was a little scared to stay there with a storm brewing and the risk that Clara and Toño wouldn't be able to make it back. *If they were my parents, they would have taken me*, I thought angrily, before I slumped down onto the cushions in the living room. Not a single light was on anywhere in the house. I tried to turn on the radio, but the rain had cut off the electricity. It was the perfect moment to accomplish what I had come for: the thunder, the house in shadows, the raindrops growing dense and constant. Besides, the only thing I could think about was my surroundings—but now, having reached the threshold of paradise, I was afraid.

I ran to my room and looked for something to throw on so I could catch up with them in town. I couldn't open the door, and right then the portion of roof that covered my room collapsed. Rather than drizzle, what was now falling onto my bed and my clothing was a heavy downpour. Absurdly, I tried to rescue a sweater that, until then, had been in my suitcase, but I only managed to get all my clothes soaking wet, so I went back to what was still the inside of the house and wrapped myself in the terry cloth robe Clara used after her showers. That's when I saw Michelle's silhouette in the doorway. Just her expression was enough for me to understand what was happening, and I led her to the living room, where there was still a little heat, and sat her down next to me on one of the floor cushions.

"My mother died this morning," she said, and she

didn't speak again for the rest of the night.

I knew that in that moment the longest hug wouldn't have been enough. I couldn't find the right thing to say, but I didn't want her to think this silence was like the others, when I'd refused to answer her on the roof. So I opened the part of the bathrobe covering my left breast, the pointy teat of a skinny animal, and I let her come close. She took it in her mouth, a thin, cold mouth, a fish mouth, as if from there she could siphon the strength she would need to get rid of her fear. For many hours, her tears wet the part of my body I hated the most.

Clara and Toño showed up later, when there were only crumbs left in the box of Havana cookies. They'd heard what had happened in town, so as soon as they came inside, they gave Michelle, who was no longer crying, a couple of hugs and a few pats on the back. The storm didn't last for several days, but it did rain again the next morning. In the morning, Toño went into town to call Mexico. From what he said when he got back, I figured out he'd spoken with the embassy, and that same night there'd be someone waiting for Michelle at the port. While he was gone, the three of us packed up clothing and rescued some things from my room. Clara made at least fifteen cups of tea, and between us, we finished off the chamomile and Michelle's last few cigarettes.

The French girl left Santa Helena almost the same

way she'd arrived: she stepped onto the dock alone
and barefoot amid the tumult of vendors. Not long
after, we went home, with all the things we'd taken
for the house and without Toño and Clara having finished repairing the roof above my room. That whole
summer, I never gained entrance to True Solitude,
that undesirable paradise, but I saw it up close, in
Michelle's blue eyes as the boat that would carry her
to the port drifted away from the dock. I watched her
for several minutes, until the boat was no more than
a glint on the sea, and for years, I saw her whenever
I remembered Santa Helena. Now, in the midst of
all the clamor of aunts and clinking teaspoons, everyone shouting all at once, I sometimes recognize her in
a face, but I don't say anything, because when these
topics come up at my family table, it's best not to
single anyone out.

Petals

I could never figure out the right way to get close to La Flor. Nor was I able to walk away from her in time, while it was still possible to trade her story out for another, one that would have taken me far from the neighborhood she frequented—those streets where the university came up against Tiber Avenue, scattered with cafés, smoke, and idle chatter. Years ago, they say, the avenue was small, but even in my childhood its name had become irritating—poorly suited to the long, noisy vulgarity that divides the area in two. According to the locals, there was nothing river-like about it, except for the flow of cars and the tall concrete bridges that freight trucks would cross to get on the highway.

As you go deeper in, the streets begin to change; they have the same desolate small-town atmosphere as the outskirts of the city where I was born. In earlier years, I'd spend hours getting lost there, turning corners hung with ivy, scanning the cozy restaurants with

wrought-iron balconies and geraniums in their windows, sometimes joining the drifters who even today
make their way from the east in May, when the heat
becomes unbearable, and raid the dumpsters when the
kitchen workers come out to empty the last vestiges
of the night. Though we never spoke, I felt a kind of
affectionate complicity toward them. I admired their
way of turning any place in the neighborhood into an
intimate space, into a home that was dirty but always
open for any business.

The best time to go to the restaurants was when
they were at their busiest, when nobody noticed my
presence and I could acquaint myself with the area's
public restrooms, which, at my twenty-odd years,
were still as novel as the proximity of women. It wasn't
strange, then, that I liked to go to the ladies' room and
immerse myself in their traces. The other bathrooms,
those intended for my sex, seemed less promising. In
the trails left in the urinals, I encountered arrogance,
sometimes rivalry, but nothing worth remembering
after arriving back at my studio, where the only way I
could survive the stench of solitude and confinement
was to take refuge in the smells I'd gathered during the
day. "The Rathole," I called it, so proud back then of
the squalor I affected.

The women's bathrooms had the charm of something new, always filled with little conversations left
behind in the mirrors, in the smears of lipstick. Perhaps

out of shyness or due to the olfactory calling that from then on would govern my life, instead of spending my evenings looking for a party or unzipping skirts in the uncomfortable seats of some movie theater, I chose to discover women in the only place where they don't feel observed: bathroom stalls. There, when one learns to read the signs, the merest trickle of liquid running down a white wall can reveal a nervous breakdown or recent upset. There was always some discovery, some new reaction that made me feel the euphoria of an apprentice, but among all those unknowns, those challenges that inspired me to play the role of interpreter, none confounded me more than La Flor.

Now, with the passage of time, of what optimists call experience but which really is no more than a kind of mildew, a salt residue capable of covering everything with rust, I can't help but smile at the absurdity of the name, not without a little self-condescension. That afternoon, when I first discovered a trace of her in Café Colón, one of those restaurants with geraniums in the windows, calling her La Flor seemed inevitable. I'd taken the avenue into the neighborhood, gone up the street with the outdoor market, and turned right at the park, having seen that the restaurant was full. The customers were trying so hard to get tables that I had no trouble entering the women's room. A trace of her in the first stall immediately drew my attention: in the white curvature of the toilet bowl, a young woman and a vague damp smell had left brown stains so slight that, if I hadn't entered, any new visitor would have erased them. The stains, as fragile as an old wrinkled face, ended up scaring me. My face still turned toward the water in the toilet, I tried to imagine her, but it was useless. It was like looking at a knot and finding no place to begin untying it. The only thing I could think of was unzipping my fly and urinating carefully on the three circles until the tile bore only my own smell, orange and penetrating. Then I was alone, without a street or a toilet where I could find her again. If I'd seen her leave, she might have turned into a thin young girl walking out of a café at midday, or the daughter of a squat red-haired man. But since that didn't happen, I felt bound to pursue her stains and smells—all that I could recognize of La Flor—and to discover, through them, the cause of her paleness, of a fragility so great I could only imagine her leaning against any surface, on the verge of collapse.

That week I went back to Café Colón every night. The urine I found was banal: minor binges, green and unimaginative; tired bladders; the occasional wild scene. I waited. I waited for hours and came back several days in a row. Until I was convinced that La Flor had no reason to return: people tend to hold certain places sacred, and frequenting them means wearing out the memory. There was also the possibility that La Flor had entered the restaurant that night only to use the bathroom. And so I decided to search the local area, out in the street, in the restrooms of other places.

Over the following days, I visited several locations. First, I took the streets leading down to the bridge, on the left side of Tiber Avenue if you're going south to north, the side where the bakery is. Again and again, I walked past the entrance to the park, stopping to look at the drifters who, by that time, always have their guitars out and are singing songs in their unintelligible language. Just like every other year, the sight of the girls with long reddish hair, the ones I could never quite approach, brought me to a standstill near the group. But that summer, maybe for the first time, I didn't linger behind the bushes at the edge of the park. That summer, I devoted myself to pursuing another woman, one I imagined in fragments, with great difficulty. That summer, I couldn't help peering into every café I passed, carefully examining each face and skin tone. Something, possibly the sadness in the stains I had seen in the toilet, made me think of La Flor's eyes as an unmistakable ashen gray. When I finally settled on a place, I would go inside pretending to look for a group of friends, and when I found no trace of her, I would leave, feigning surprise and feeling a deep unease. This method seemed to be effective.

Saturday, before ten, I came across the second sign. I found it in a diner on the other side of the avenue. I went directly to the ladies' room, much more modest than the first. Now color was almost entirely absent from her traces, as if she were asleep, or maybe crazy. But the smell was very strong: sour sweat against a backdrop of wine and the tedium of old age, someone living a few extra hours. In spite of all this and the shape of her stains, long and plain like fish excrement, I convinced myself she wasn't ill, that her body's weakness had another source.

"Too much booze," I said out loud, with frustration, as if predicting the ending of a movie. A woman in the next stall cried out in a shrill voice that a man was in the bathroom. I was a little alarmed but decided to pay no attention. I checked the lock and let my eyes rest for a few minutes on the bottom of the toilet bowl, not just because I wanted to take full advantage of my finding, but also because I realized I liked to feel her near me, both as an object of analysis and as something about to appear: an eclipse or a war among butterflies that I'd be lucky enough to witness. Luckily, there were almost no customers that day, and no one heard the lady, who rushed out of the bathroom without washing her hands. A few minutes later, I climbed out of the window above the sinks and went to sit on some steps near the avenue, where my strength slowly waned. The scent of wine could have been enough to disillusion me, but I still wasn't able to calm down. That evening, surrounded by the roar of traffic, I understood that sometimes there is only one door, that even if I wanted to, I wouldn't be able to escape from this story through a back window. In some barely perceptible way, I sensed that my duty was to find her and dissuade her from something I couldn't even define, something I myself might have been inventing. I looked at the avenue and saw at least five restaurants I hadn't yet visited. It was too late to examine them all before they closed. I stood up as best I could and walked off so I wouldn't get stuck there brooding.

It took me a long time to find a convincing place, but after walking the whole neighborhood, I came to the brightly lit door of Mazarin. I felt so exhausted I almost left without going inside. There was no reason to think that La Flor would be in a place like this— so much more expensive than the others, and, at that hour, almost empty of customers—but I made the effort nonetheless. I crossed the threshold, scrutinizing two floors decorated with plants, the terrace where a fountain of luminous green water accompanied the last few conversations. Then I looked for the bathroom to see if I could find some clue that would justify my vigilance. I went inside quickly, making sure that no one saw me.

At least once in his life, every olfactorist must surely experience a moment of plenitude like the one I experienced in the ladies' room of Mazarin. I don't know if my ecstasy was inspired by the discreet marble furniture and flooring, the high ceiling that allowed smells to circulate freely, or the spacious stall I meticulously searched. The best atmospheres are like states of mind, they can be sensed but not interpreted, and though I would recognize the exact tone of the indirect lighting, the murmur of the voices outside, and the plants that were everywhere, even in the bathroom, all that remains for me of that environment is a faded nostalgia, like the glow of a beautiful, distant memory. The bathroom was a miniature copy of the restaurant itself. Just bending over the toilet, you were met with the smells of the dishes, the blintzes or the duck in mango sauce. But the best part was that from there, with your face almost inside the bowl, you could breathe in more than the ingredients: the pleasure of the diners, the way each one had interpreted the taste of breakfast or dinner the night before. Among the variety of tiny stains—the toilet appeared to remain clean the whole night—I found the timid traces of my flower, La Flor. It was easy for me to distinguish them from others, firstly because there were very few others, and secondly, because what was left was so ephemeral, the same transient green as before, but this time distributed around the basin. It was as if her whole life had slipped out from deep inside her. The image struck me as so intense that I had to raise my face for a few seconds to breathe. Where had this woman found the energy to leave the bathroom? Everything was there, and I had no idea how to decipher it. I couldn't see anything in the tile except my impotence, my ineptitude. Something fell into the depths of the water; something damp and transparent fell again and again, wetting my face with a salty, shameful taste.

Amid the confusion, all I could do was hold on to the traces before me: La Flor hadn't eaten a thing since the night before. Beneath the usual weakness, I noticed exhaustion—this time physical—and a thirst lasting several hours, which rusted her lips, the only lips I could imagine and which served as a model for her tiny, sensuous mouth. Outside, the hum of people softened, making way for the sound of the water. I thought of her, imagined her stubbornly biting her nails in front of a green lake all lit up like the central fountain in the restaurant.

A little calmer now, I looked down and then away at least three times. The longer I stared at the backsplash, the more chaos took hold of the traces, reshaping them as in a deranged kaleidoscope. In my second reading, La Flor had several possible bodies. I had doubts about the size of her mouth, and the tones of her urine even disgusted me, the certainty that her whole self had begun to decay. I stood up suddenly and left the bathroom, indignant, thinking that La Flor deserved more respect. If I weren't able to help her, I certainly had no right to inspect her dark recesses. It was late. I walked in the direction of the bridge, keeping my head down, and waited for a bus that would take me back to my rathole—which, more than ever, is what it was that night.

In bed, I missed the warmth of the first stains and pictured myself dancing with her in the park, very close, our noses almost touching, while someone sang a song in a summery language. But I had no time to enjoy the dream: in a few hours—if it hadn't already happened—I would lose my chance to find her forever. I turned on the desk lamp and, leaning back against the wall, counted the money I had in a drawer to see if, assuming it wasn't too late, I could ask her out to dinner with what was left of my last paycheck. I would have liked to spend a night with La Flor, to enter the world of her habits without telling her anything at first, and later to surprise her little by little with all the things I knew about her. I turned off the light to let the morning finish spilling into the window of my room.

That afternoon, I went back to Mazarin and spent almost an hour in the first stall without success. In the toilet stains, I found nothing of her, not even the vestiges of her last visit. Before ten, when most restaurants in the neighborhood close their doors, I left my hiding place and ran desperately out into the street, going into every bathroom I could find: one clue, one single sign would have reassured me.

I know now that in situations like this it doesn't help to spend so much time looking, that it's better to think before moving around, to analyze, almost like a visionary, the evidence within reach. But that's not what I did that night. That night, I inspected all the toilets I had before me, all the mirrors, all the traces. In my hasty tour of the neighborhood, I returned to Mazarin at least three times before discovering a round little earring covered in soap in one of the shiny white sinks there. I knew by the smell, by the tiny amber stone threaded rustically onto a silver wire. For years afterward I could feel that hoop between my fingers, as if I were still toying with its slippery fragility above the drain of the sink. I didn't go out again that night. I chose the cowardly consolation of uncertainty instead.

There was a little ventilation grille up near the ceiling. I locked the door—at that hour, the restaurant was full—and climbed up on to the sinks to look out: the scene outside calmed me. Perhaps it was the dusky twilight or the everyday image of the bridge, its flow of cars the most intense it would be all day, but I felt sure she would return for her earring. I unlocked the door and went back to the stall to wait, crouching on the floor beside the toilet. The waiting period was filled with other women. In all the months I'd spent tracking stains and odors, I'd never been present for the moment of production, when various tints drip onto the tile and paint their stories. So I tried to entertain myself watching a dozen buttocks and raised skirts move through the neighboring stalls, but each time the door opened I felt yet another surge of disappointment, deepening the furrow in my mood. After two hours or maybe much longer—I couldn't say, exactly—La Flor returned.

It wasn't hard to recognize her: her odor entered the bathroom before she did and took the air by force. I listened to her walk in front of the mirrors and pause at painful, endless places until, probably more by chance than any impulse of her own, she put her hand on the lock of the next stall over. I was too agitated to take a look. In that moment, while I bit down hard on the earring with my incisors to keep from crying out, La Flor was with me, murmuring a slow, sweet waterfall, much more pleasurable than the nearness of any other body. I don't know how long I stayed sitting there. I think it took her a while to pull up her loose-fitting jeans. I kept hidden until she left the stall, and then went out a little later, when I calculated she'd have arrived in the lobby. We left the restaurant—I want to use that verb in the first person plural, though the truth is I was following her, without daring to stop her. It still seemed important that I change the direction she was walking in, but I was no longer hounded by an anxious urgency. The night air was almost cool, and a wind was blowing from the east; I thought about how the festivities in the park would soon be over.

She—I can no longer refer to her by the same name as before walked with her hands in the pockets of a worn sweatshirt. Her long reddish braid moved like a pendulum across her back, and each step she took seemed determined by the avenue's old and terrifyingly familiar path. I didn't follow her for that long, nor did I dare to accompany her up the steps of the bridge. With the same fear that, for so many nights, had kept me away from the dances in front of the hostel, I simply watched her lean over the handrail, toward the hum of the cars. I watched her for a long time, long enough to have reached her if I had hurried. But I didn't go up after her. I didn't do it even when the inventory of stains and smells seemed so clear, as easy to grasp as the way she walked. Perhaps I didn't do it out of fear, or maybe because I didn't recognize anything familiar in her face, which I remember very little of, except that her eyes were neither gray nor unmistakable. I looked compulsively out toward the flow of the Tiber as I spun the earring around on the tip of my index finger, but with only a slight shiver, that remote pity aroused by any stranger's misfortune, when her swaying on the bridge turned into those last few traces, petals on the pavement, which the cars did not dare to crush.

Bezoar

Another supposed cure-all I had to contend with was the bezoar stone. These stones are secretions found in the stomachs of animals that devour their own hair, especially in a certain goat in India, and it is said that they prevent melancholy and jaundice and serve as an antidote against all sorts of poisons.

AMBROISE PARÉ
Les discours

In spite of all my reservations, I've decided to begin keeping this absurd journal once and for all. Since our first consultation, you've insisted on the importance of noting down any memories and impressions that emerge while I'm here. I have to admit that this place is wonderful, close to the sea, far from any kind of tensions, except the ones I constantly inflict on myself. It's so beautiful and quiet that, more than a rehab clinic, it feels like a seaside resort. From my room, whose window faces the cliff, I can see the slightest changes in the landscape, though I'm convinced that this kind of detail, important for me, will be totally irrelevant to the reader of this damn diary (forgive me, Doctor, but if I don't try to unwind a little, nothing will come out of my pen). I've never kept a journal like this, so I don't really know where to start. Maybe on the day when my condition forced me to check myself into this sanatorium, or the moment I started swallowing all sorts of hallucinogens now replaced by the tranquilizers you supply me with, Dr. Murillo, to ease my compulsive tendencies. I hate to let you down. Though it's true that here, it's almost impossible to use drugs, at least unless you've prescribed them, you still haven't managed to banish the beast. Allow me to explain: the compulsion didn't begin the moment I smoked my first innocent joint, or when it was impossible for me to stop masturbating, a phase my sister mentioned during the consultation and that you brought up again at our last appointment. It manifested years earlier, in the form of a habit you can't even imagine, much less try to cure. I wonder how much time I'll spend in this isolated Eden before you understand the real problem and that everything else is just the consequence of a simple, though not completely inoffensive, childhood gesture.

I was nine years old. Months earlier, my parents had announced their imminent divorce—I mention this fact to humor you, since I know all too well the importance you grant coincidences like these, although, to be frank, it seems like a psychologist's superstition to me, the same way painters never walk under ladders and taxi drivers swerve to avoid black cats. I guess each profession has its own.

It was one of those sunny mornings in June when it took no effort at all to get up for school; the minutes even seemed longer than usual. My sister Luisa and I were doing our hair in front of the mirror on my mother's dressing table, my sister with the never-ending braids of a two-faced little girl, I with reddish eighties-style bangs. Undecided about which clothes she'd put on that morning, my mother ran about from one end of the room to the other like a fly looking for an escape route and smashing against the windows instead. During one of these comings and goings, it occurred to her to stop and evaluate her daughters. In the mirror, her disapproving gaze landed on my bangs for a few seconds. "If you keep combing your hair like that," she warned, "those bangs are going to plaster your whole forehead." I raised my hair to check and confirmed that my forehead had shrunk to half its original size. At least, that's how it seemed to me then. My mother had finished putting on her makeup more than ten minutes earlier, but it was still out on the dressing table: the open mascara, the blush brush out of its case, and the golden tweezers, which, for some reason, I'd

always been drawn to. I held them carefully between
my fingers and began to pull out the hairs that I felt
had invaded my forehead. I remember that pulling
them out made me feel indescribably relieved, as if each
one had come to represent a problem.

That morning, I also learned about the anatomy of
a hair. I discovered that, aside from the external aspect
we all know, there is a slimy, hidden part that forms
the root. This part triggered in me an animal aversion.
It wasn't repulsion, but a kind of loathing, and also the
need to get rid of it as soon as possible. The first thing
I thought of was to put the follicle in my mouth and
swallow it. Perhaps because it came from inside my
body, it seemed natural that I return it to its unfath-
omable origins. All this happened very fast, but the act
wasn't limited to that morning. During the day, despite
the fact that I didn't have the tweezers, I repeated the
procedure several times with the tips of my fingers,
which at that time were awkward and lacked the skill
they'd develop over the years. Who would have guessed
that this casual gesture was the start of a lifelong habit?
If my mother had suspected it, she never would have
let the tweezers fall into my hands. Most likely, when
she did notice, she thought it was just one of my usual
fleeting eccentricities and that I'd forget all about it in a
week or so. But, for some reason I can't name, it didn't
happen that way.

From then on, every time I had some difficulty at

school, every time the teacher explained some incomprehensible grammar rule or I got lost in the aimless labyrinth of algebra, I'd return to the ritual like someone taking shelter, someone under a spell. It was a way of disconnecting from the world, of turning my back on the life in which I definitively did not want to participate.

When you read this, Doctor, you'll probably wonder why I don't show any visible sign of this fixation. My tonsured period didn't last long. It was too embarrassing to be caught in action when I wasn't discreet enough (sometimes I didn't even have time to run to the bathroom), and even worse to be called "baldy" or "the mad monk." So I learned to better distribute the sites of extraction. It's true that some spots were more pleasurable than others. The gratification of pulling out a hair varies according to the area it comes from, hence the risk of making holes, but with a little exploration, you end up finding pleasure where you'd least expect it. Legs, for example, turn out to be an inexhaustible mine in moments of bulimia, but they're not even remotely my favorite. There are much more irresistible places, including the tip of the chin, where a little hair grows, thick and all on its own. The excitement I feel when I pull it out is so great that I've been tempted to shave my chin to see if others of the same category will grow there.

October 19

Perhaps, Dr. Murillo, you think talking about hair is
just a way of avoiding the subject of addiction. I, on the
other hand, am convinced it's the origin, where everything comes from, the mother of vice, you might say. If
you pay close attention, you'll see I've changed compulsions a great number of times: I started smoking when
I stopped drinking, I abandoned marijuana when I discovered the euphoria of cocaine, and the latter seemed
innocuous when I stumbled upon the holy joy of Ecstasy.
But even so, not a single day has passed without my
pulling out a hair, not even in this place where nothing
should worry me. Yesterday, for example, while trying
to decide if I should or shouldn't tell you about this, I
fell into one of those moments of trance. In the course
of these last few pages, I started to play with my curls,
and, when I least intended to, I fell back into the act. I
noticed that I was moving the pen over the page without
writing anything. *I should tell Dr. Murillo about this as
soon as possible*, I thought, but something in me, maybe
that antisocial rebelliousness you've mentioned, refused
to admit it. *I won't say anything*, answered the other side
of my persona. *This will be the one private space I keep for
myself.* While I was thinking, strands of hair fell on the
notebook like the leaves of my own personal autumn.
I searched for an appetizing one on my head and took
it between my fingers: *This is the last one*, I promised

myself. *If it comes out with the root, I'll tell Murillo; if not, I'll keep up the silent battle.* I pulled hard on the hair and looked at the result: the root was enormous, but the consequences seemed unbearable, so I decided to try again. It took time to find another sample that attractive. My arm was getting tired of searching. When it finally appeared, I repeated the action mechanically, but on this occasion, there was no bulb on the tip. The hair was a continuous thread. *Two out of three*, I said to myself. *The third will be the deal breaker.* The next time a root came out again, though smaller than the first.

I think I only stopped because my arm hurt so much from holding what my sister called the "monkey position." In my window, the sun was setting, which is how I realized I'd been trying to decide for many hours. My shoulders and neck were tense and aching. I gathered up the hairs on the table and put them in the desk drawer.

October 22

I return to the diary feeling ashamed. In spite of my resolution, I couldn't bring myself to mention the matter this morning. I have to say, Doctor, you didn't leave me much space, but sooner or later I'll have to tell you. Just as you stick to your scientist's conclusions, I've given myself one rule: never contradict the oracle of hair.

October 25

You're now asking me to expound on biographical details, especially those related to Victor. Before I talk about him, or rather, about our unfortunate encounter, I need to put him in context. I'm guessing, Dr. Murillo, that besides satisfying your curiosity, writing this will help remove a layer of dust from the chaotic archive my memory has become. I'm convinced that we ended up where we did for reasons encoded in a series of seemingly minor events, and I'll attempt to recall them here. Besides, I predict that this journal may be useful in the future, especially if I'm faced with some hearing, either before a court of law or my own family.

I'll comment on the beginnings of my adolescence, a particularly onerous time for anyone, but especially for those who are somehow different from their peer group. At that time, I had no idea how to control my movements. I would repeat the action several times a minute. Not even a shadow of willpower was left. Like the survivor of a shipwreck, dragged by the whims of the waves, I let myself be swept along by habit. I constantly felt humiliated, victimized by an abuse I inflicted on myself without knowing why. Nothing was under my control, not the when or the where of the crises, which consisted of pulling out entire locks of hair instead of just one. As I've said before, during this period, I exhibited bald spots of varying sizes, and though I tried to hide them under my John Lennon cut, I didn't have enough hair to cover the disgrace. At that point, "combing my hair" was a matter of choosing which bald spots to cover and which to leave in sight.

It was hard for my parents to take me out in public. Bringing me to temple or family reunions was a shameful experience for them. When they saw me, people would act like they didn't notice, but it was so obvious that even the most clueless among them would realize it. In short, a wooden atmosphere was built up around me, that characteristic artificiality discomfort provokes. Since I was still just a little girl—I've always looked younger than I am—the inquisitive eyes would immediately fall on my progenitors, as if people needed at least an explanation to accept my abnormality. It just wasn't possible for someone my age to be so nervous. My parents must have played some role in it, if not caused it entirely. Cornered, they took refuge in Luisa, who, besides being conventional, was very feminine and a good student. They'd put her in front of me and spend the rest of the day enumerating her virtues.

More than the feeling of being ruled by an impulse I couldn't control, what affected my behavior most during those years was the way people looked at me. The other children were afraid or even contemptuous, and the adults didn't seem to trust me. From someone like me, you could expect practically anything. This opinion of me was so unanimous that even I ended up accepting it. Friends of the family, distant enough to tolerate what was happening, assured my parents that time would work in their favor. It was just a matter of my getting through adolescence.

I remember that around that time a book on myths and legends fell into my hands. In it, there was a drawing of a woman with hair down to her waist, holding a wonderful gemstone in her hand. According to the author of that book, in a place very far from our continent, there was a stone or ball of hair with healing powers. The bezoar was the remedy for all poisons and also the stone of perfect calm. This discovery disturbed me. First, because it seemed hard to believe that a precious gem could be confused with a ball of hair. On the other hand, there was something about the legend that made sense: I pulled my hair out because when I did, I was lavished with perfect calm and tranquility, if only for a fraction of a second.

October 30

Stormy night.

Yesterday, after dinner, I spent several minutes in the hospital dining room, hypnotized by the big windows. The sea seemed to be coming right at us. I couldn't help thinking about Victor, whom I haven't heard from in over a month. Is he still here? It scares me to ask the question out loud. During our last session, you asked if I still feel capable of carrying out an impulsive act. Allow me to stop writing for a moment and laugh. Doctor, every moment of my life, this very instant included, I struggle to choose from a shower of possibilities, which you would call irrational and which I feel are the most tempting in the world. For example, half an hour ago, when the nurse knocked on the door announcing that she had my evening medication, I wondered whether or not I should break the chair over her head. It's not that I have any complaints about her; on the contrary, she's a very kind, helpful woman, but sometimes the mere fact that she exists is enough to infuriate me. The day you passed me the note with Victor's unmistakable handwriting in the return address, I vacillated between throwing myself out the window right then and there, or waiting until the hospital lights went off to do it, so my last image would be of the lighthouse shining on the bay. When you've allowed yourself to be controlled for so long by actions you don't recognize as your own but that also don't belong to anyone else's mind, when you've loosened the sphincter of your willpower to such an extent that you have no idea what you'll do from one minute to the next, you're even less sure whether your actions would qualify as "irresponsible." But, like wrinkles and other imperfections of the skin, you learn how to conceal these defects. And something tells me

you know this better than anyone. I'll return to the
story of my life so you understand me better.

By the time I was seventeen, I'd become an expert at
pretending. If I wasn't completely normal, at least I no
longer suffered those shameful moments when I lost
all self-control. I kept pulling out my hair—I hadn't
missed a single day since that morning in front of my
mother's dressing table—but I had learned to hide it.
My consciousness had become a box of tricks and sim-
ulation techniques. Instead of my eighties hairstyle, I
now wore my reddish hair long, with enough volume
that no one could have imagined there were completely
hairless patches underneath.

I could, for example, spend the whole night chatting
with a friend at a table in some restaurant without her
or any other diner noticing my movements; I'd listen
without interruption as my companion mused about
the summer's fashions and the abysmal differences
that, according to her, were distancing her from her
boyfriend, and at the same time surrender completely
to my vice.

Only at the end of the night, after taking our plates
and sweeping under the table, would the waiter discover a reddish trail, the kind that forms around a
hairdresser's chair, but by then, it didn't matter. I would
leave the restaurant happy, my only thoughts of con-
tinuing the party. I had turned into a functional being,
which, believe me, was the ultimate achievement of my

entire existence. Anyone who has come out of a swamp of infamy like the one where I spent my childhood will recognize the sensation of relief produced by going unnoticed. You might wonder, then, what brought me to the state I was in—edgy, sleepless, skeletal—when I made it here, to this clinic. I'm getting there, Doctor, but I don't want to leave out any important details, so you'll have to be patient.

As I explained before, my social integration was a triumph superior to all others, and I can say that when I attained it, my personality radically changed. I became extroverted, a girl surrounded by friends and admirers. Even my sister Luisa paled next to the charisma I radiated during those years. My skill for seduction came from the inexhaustible mine of frustrations I needed to make up for, and because of that, it was nothing less than devastating. When I started college, I got a job with a modeling agency, and my reddish mane advertised shampoo and other hair products on TV. I liked parties, and the work at the agency complemented that penchant. It's not that I made millions, but it was certainly enough to reassure my parents about my future. In appearance, my life was like any other. Nevertheless, it lacked something that almost no one can do without, something that at the beginning I didn't need but that I ended up missing without even realizing it: intimacy. I had totally forbidden myself honest, trusting relationships. I knew exactly how it felt to be talked about by everyone, and there was nothing in the world that would make me willing to run that risk. The friend to whom you confide your most secret dreams and sorrows would only ever be a figment of my imagination. Even though I liked some of the boys who were after me enough to go out with, my relationships with them were limited to chance encounters, generally late at night and in situations of extreme drunkenness. I don't know how long I could have gone on like this, maybe my whole life, and in fact, maybe that would have been prudent. As arbitrary as they may seem from the outside, those rules sustained my existence, and to infringe upon them would have meant annihilating the order of survival. But rules, an old proverb says, are meant to be broken, remember, Dr. Murillo? And I, like many who understand the unique forms of their vital equilibrium, felt tempted to pull out the nail holding up the entire mess.

It happened the day I met Victor Ghica, whom my friends nicknamed Rumanovich for his Moldavian last name and origins. Victor worked with the same agency as I did. His main field was underwear. I had seen his naked torso in several of the magazines I appeared in, and on ads in the street, and I'd promised myself I would sink my teeth into him. I didn't care that he was known for being abusive and depraved. I always moved on before anyone got the better of me. So it was only a matter of finding the right place and time.

It was the end of the summer, during a party at Dance Palace. I'd spent the whole night perched on the wall of a terrace, accepting every dry martini my male friends brought over to me and tossing olive pits over the edge. I was wearing a flowery, knee-length cotton skirt. The tan on my legs was at its peak. The reason why I hadn't moved from the terrace was twofold: there were fewer people there—I could set my drink on the railing without asking anyone to hold it or having to fight for space—and, with my back to the ledge, no one could stand behind me and watch as strands of my hair fell into the abyss. The city view was a true delight, and the sea air soothed our sun-scorched skin. I wouldn't have moved from there all night if I hadn't spotted Victor Ghica among those milling around inside.

When I saw him come in, I was already so drunk that I didn't bother coming up with some original pretext for my approach. I walked toward the main room as well as I could and made a place for myself next to him at the bar. I took a cigarette from my purse and followed rule number one of the most rudimentary pickup manual:

"Do you have a light?" I asked, looking into his eyes.

Rumanovich smiled and slid his hand into his pocket. He took out a silver lighter and, before lighting it, made a strange movement with his fingers. His knuckles cracked as the flame appeared. I told myself the man had style. Victor called the bartender over and asked for a beer. Afterward, he looked over at me and asked:

"Can I get you a martini?"

As he followed me out to the terrace, he wasted no time in insisting that he'd noticed me at a few parties.

In person, Rumanovich didn't look much like his image in photos. While in the underwear ads he had the brash sensuality of a bull, self-assured and overpowering, in real life he seemed withdrawn, almost tense. He looked like a nerdy kid because of his glasses, and also because of the way he measured his words when he spoke. Our first night together, he explained that his work with the agency was just a way to earn a living and that his real passion was philosophy. He was different from the other boys who modeled. When I really think about it, he was different from anyone else I'd ever met.

On the terrace, I went back to my original position, and while he talked about school and his projects, I gave in to my favorite vice, this time with double the discretion. Something about this man was driving me crazy, maybe his way of questioning the world I moved through, the look in his eyes, too inquisitive for my taste, or the way he drummed his fingers. All that restlessness intensified my compulsions.

We spent the night in the Palace's greenhouse, next to a planter containing different species of cactus. I remember we lay and waited for daybreak among the plants. We smoked a couple of cigarettes while we watched the sun paint the plastic curtains red. My skirt was stained with semen and my tanned thighs showed traces of dirt.

"Do you like cacti?" Rumanovich asked.

"I don't think so," I said, shrugging.

"How strange. I thought you'd love them."

I took another puff of my cigarette and let the smoke vanish slowly in the morning cold before answering.

"Oh really? You thought that?" I asked. "And why might that be?"

"I'm not sure," he said. "Maybe because of the thorns."

I drew back the plastic curtain to leave the greenhouse and stretched my arms with a theatrical yawn.

Victor took me back to my house in his car. When we arrived, they had already taken his photo down from the bus stop.

Despite what you might think, Dr. Murillo, I had no intention of seeing Victor again. That morning I got out of his car a block before my house, and when we said goodbye, I gave him a fake number. It's not that I didn't like him—on the contrary, I've already told you I found him mysterious and attractive—but the rule was, no man had the right to more than one chance, and even less so if he was sober.

"I'll call you on Sunday," Rumanovich promised romantically at the door of my supposed building. The only response I gave him was a limp smile, the same one I'd used in the Pantene commercial. When he left, I walked home. I remember I was diabolically hungover on both Saturday and Sunday. I was especially tormented by having pulled out so much hair at the party. When I got out of the shower, it seemed that not even the best extra-volume mousse could save me. I would be out of circulation for a few months, until the roots grew again: a suicidal decision considering that the agency had hired me less than a year ago. And the more I thought about it, the more I fell into the shameful act.

On Sunday, I didn't take any phone calls. I told my mother I had a headache and locked myself in my room. But late that afternoon, she couldn't hold back any longer and came upstairs to knock on my door:

"It's the sixth time this guy has called. He says if you don't answer, he's going to come here to see you."

I couldn't believe it. Rumanovich had found my number and probably also had the right address.

I had no doubt that he would carry out his threat, so I took the phone to tell him to go to hell.

I ended up having dinner with him that same Sunday, in a Japanese restaurant on Calle Londres. Victor looked even more nervous that night, though no less handsome.

Before the food came, he put his cards on the table:

"I know you like me," he began in a falsely velvety voice. "It's clear from a mile away."

(Evasive silence on my part.)

"I like you, too, and I want you to be my girl."

(This time, a sarcastic but discreet smile.)

"I know you're always decapitating your lovers"—who could have told him?—"but that will never work with me."

I chose a friendly strategy, and in the warmest and most "intimate" tone I could muster, I said I was sorry but that for reasons I couldn't explain, I couldn't have a boyfriend. I assured him that he was the best-looking and most interesting guy at the agency and suggested he look for a young college girl, preferably a philosophical type, one who could really understand him.

"The only one who *can understand me* is you," he said, "even though you're so clueless you still don't realize it."

"But the thing is, I don't want to *understand you*," I said to him, losing my patience. "I swear to god"—we were always saying that then—"you better not push it."

They brought the sushi. Rumanovich picked up the chopsticks with his long fingers and looked at me in silence. That white shirt looked great on him. I asked him if he'd done an ad for Loewe or bought it with his own money.

"Don't change the subject," he said. "I'm here to convince you. Let's see, have you ever had a boyfriend? Not even in high school?"

"No," I answered.

"And now that you've met the love of your life, you're going to let him slip away just like that?"

"That's just your point of view," I answered. But something inside me told me that Victor was right.

"Your attitude is reasonable," he countered in the voice of a Moldavian scholar, "but whether it's in our best interests or not, there's nothing you can do about this."

I was surprised by how closely the corny Romanian style resembled the Mexican *rancheras*.

I looked at my watch. More than an hour had passed without me pulling a single hair, and to celebrate, I ordered a green-tea ice cream. We were on our third bottle of sake, and I felt the heat of the fermented rice going to my head. Victor was irresistible. What did I have to lose kissing him a few more times?

"I've been watching you for over a month," he said. "When you asked me to park in front of that building, I knew perfectly well that you didn't live there. I knew you were giving me a fake number and that you'd only agree to see me again if I threatened you somehow. I also know that if you don't want to go out with me, it's because you're afraid I'll discover that mania you have with your hair, but darling, I've known about that for a long time."

The effect of the sake vanished in a matter of seconds. Victor had turned into some sort of expressionless executioner, the personification of all my fears. I didn't say anything back. Instead, I stood up and told him I was going to the bathroom. I crossed the restaurant with the sensation that I might fall to the floor at any minute. Once I was alone, I wet my face with cold water, trying to lower its temperature, which had suddenly gone up. I lit a cigarette and weighed my few options: deny it completely and accuse him of slander, tell everyone he sexually harassed me to discredit anything he said, or cause an accident by cutting the brakes in his car. I returned with a smile on my lips and pretended to be out of my mind.

"Let's see," I began, "what was the last crazy thing you said?"

"I like how you're such a con artist," he answered, "but that won't work with me. Deep down, we're very similar. I don't pull out my hair, but I have other manias. Think about it, honey: what I'm offering you, no one else can give."

I asked him to take me home. Now I really did have a headache, and I needed some fresh air.

Victor paid the bill and handed the stub to valet parking. He had stopped talking. I didn't say a word, either. When we got to the highway, he put the top down on his car and turned the cassette player on. The Beatles blasted on the highway, but we weren't going toward my house. We were going high above the city, to the greenhouse at Dance Palace.

November 8

The year is ending. The trees in the garden are all turning red like a ridiculous extension of my long hair. I
haven't been able to quit my vice even with the pills.
Two days have passed since I got Victor's note. He says
he's been admitted to this hospital, too. He wants us
to see each other again. I don't know exactly how to
explain the way this news made me feel. The closest
words to it might be "mortal terror."

Be especially vigilant, Dr. Murillo. I don't trust his
supposedly peaceful demeanor.

November 9

Yesterday afternoon, when I came back from your
office, I ran into the woman who lives in the next
room, the one with the nose tic. Her door was open
and I could see her yelling in her bed. "Turn off the
AC," she said. "I'm freezing to death!"

Actually, it was hot. The sea breeze barely reached
the building. "When has it ever been cold in August?"
the nurse who was with me shot back. Hearing her
scream had made me feel better. I admire people who
know how to scream. "If I could scream like that," I
said to the nurse, "I probably wouldn't be here."

November 11

Victor was right when he said that he was the love of my life, and I was right, too, when I said it would be better not to start anything. Even so, three weeks later, we decided to move in together. We rented an apartment facing a park. The first days of our story now seem so distant and impossible. It's hard for me to believe that we were once happy, that the word "intimacy" might contain, during exceptional periods of existence, more than one person. I trusted Victor in a way I'd never done with anyone. Very soon, however, the disillusionment began.

Don't be confused, Doctor, our problems had nothing to do with the fact that he thought in Romanian while I thought in Spanish, nor with his passion for literature, which I didn't share one iota of, nor our eventual disagreements over the décor in the apartment. In short, our problems weren't caused by our differences but by our unavoidable similarities. Often I wasn't able to settle for the occasional, discreet extraction of a hair. Locked in the bathroom or my bedroom, I would succumb to the use of tweezers and prepare veritable banquets of hair follicles for myself. Those excesses sometimes lasted several hours. Facing the bathroom mirror or sitting on my bed with a compact in my hand, I would lay into my eyebrows, temples, armpits, whatever part of the body caught my attention at that moment. The fast pace of those months was extremely taxing—anyone who knows the modeling world would agree—and I don't know how I would have survived without those moments of release. It's not that I'd lost my sense of shame with Victor, but at least I was able to talk to him about it. He would listen to me in silence, most of the time with a cigarette in hand. His face didn't show the revolting pity mental disorders provoke in some people, but nor did he have the flippant look of someone who's completely unfamiliar with the subject. He was perfectly aware of the seriousness of the matter and also understood that it was manageable. It was such a relief to talk to him. We were like two exiles hiding out on a strange planet.

Victor's manias were also well hidden from the outside world. You had to watch him for a long time to realize that he cracked his knuckles compulsively—not to be trendy, as I'd thought at the beginning—because he did it in such a natural way, and the crackling sound was barely audible. Even so, after the first few months, that unnecessary and completely permissible act began to annoy me. Gradually, my hearing became more and more sensitive to the crackling. I would hear it from my room while he was cooking something in the kitchen. The sound of his bones reached my ears like a fatal note, too repetitive for me to tolerate. Dr. Murillo, if you or any of your students think I seem ungrateful for getting worked up over something like this, know before judging me that I endured the torture for several months without saying a word. But there came a point when I couldn't handle it anymore. Yes, I suffered sudden fits, but he lived under the constant control of his habit. At night, while we slept, the crackling of his bones marked the passage of time, in counterpoint to the alarm clock. There was not a single moment, not even during sex, when Victor stopped cracking his knuckles.

Seeing our own defects in the person we share a life with is intolerable. Can you imagine living with a nurse as hairy and sadistic as you are, Doctor? With another human walrus? You wouldn't be able to stand it, either. The problem, Dr. Murillo, is that I was in love with Victor, and even worse, I was convinced that he was the only person I could really trust, that I couldn't leave him for anything in the world.

November 12

Before leaving my room, I wait behind the peephole in my door until the hallway is empty and silent. I'm afraid of running into someone on the stairs that lead to the shower or dining room. You never know, the people who come to places like this can be friendly but also dangerous. For some time now, I've been suspicious of the human species; I prefer to keep my distance. Victor, on the other hand, wasn't afraid of people. He never cared if people noticed him cracking his knuckles or folding up little pieces of paper until they were microscopic. According to him, these obsessions were compatible with his philosopher personality, the price he paid for having his own style. I'll admit that I've always admired his audacity, but the way he acted made me very uncomfortable. A stranger revealing his dark side in public is one thing, but it's another altogether to have a freak for a boyfriend. I had been a misfit my whole childhood and had no desire to continue being associated with that kind of behavior.

Each time I heard the ominous snap, a momentary tension would appear in my face, as painful to me as his obsession was to him, and he noticed it. I don't know how to explain it, but those cracks, which at first were nothing more than slight additions to the ambient noise, began to take on a disastrous dimension. They were similar in effect to five fingernails slowly scraping down a blackboard. I know those are very different sounds and that one lasts much longer than the other, but to me, it was the same. They say water continually dripping onto the floor of a dungeon can destroy a prisoner's nerves in just a few days. I assure you, Doctor, living with someone who cracks his knuckles all the time is more or less the same thing.

I began to distance myself, to look for any excuse not to be near him. If there was a party, I'd stay home so

I could enjoy a peaceful evening without his constant noises. I started to dream of leaving him, forgetting that he existed and immersing myself in absolute silence, just like the one in this hospital, as long as the woman the next room over doesn't start shouting gibberish. Still, I wanted to talk to him, to see if there was something we could do to save the relationship.

We tried as hard as we could, and although we were largely successful in reducing the frequency of our own symptoms, it wasn't enough to help us put up with each other. Just as I could hear each and every one of his snaps—even from several yards away—he would notice when I had the urge to pull out a hair even before I began doing it. We were always ready to pounce, devoted to exercising censorship and, at the same time, trying to escape it. But neither of us could stand the domestic repression, much less the self-policing.

After several months of this maddening dynamic, I thought of seeking professional help: if we wanted to stay together, we had to stand our ground and be open to even the most humiliating solutions.

We thought of various options and subjected ourselves to several, even attending group therapy through Compulsives Anonymous. But all our attempts ended in failure. Those kinds of groups are built on mutual understanding between the participants, but almost all the other members of the one we joined were smokers, drug addicts, or compulsive eaters. Our tics seemed like a joke to them; they couldn't believe anyone would be addicted to such things. I suggested we see a specialist, but Victor refused. His parents had dragged him from one shrink to another for his whole childhood without finding a single scientific solution to what he considered his originality.

That summer, however, brought a new source of hope: our neighbor gave us a bottle of his "special recipe," a mixture of several strains of marijuana and a touch of mescaline. The concoction turned out to be an immediate remedy. The marijuana not only made both of us less aware of each other's compulsions, but also relaxed us and busied us with a series of fantasies, greatly reducing the frequency of our tics. From June to September, Victor and I lived in blessed peace. Our house recovered the celebratory atmosphere of the early days. But sooner or later, the panacea would run out. Victor, who in general tends to be cautious, had begun rationing the mixture in the middle of August. Even so, by the beginning of September, the little bottle contained no more than the scent of those calm, irretrievable days. In vain, we begged the neighbor to sell us a little more of his miracle potion: the crop was depleted.

So we moved on to mescaline in powder form, but we could never figure the dosage out, which triggered some moments of real panic. Pure marijuana didn't have the same effect, either. It was desperation, Doctor, and not vice, as you and my family believe, that led us to consume so many different substances. Victor and I were looking for something that would enable us to keep living together, that's all. The neighbor's marijuana was our epilogue, the brief moment of strength that the dying experience in their final days.

November 15

You urge me to finish with the diary so we can move on to the follow-up interview. I have no problem telling you how things went, but I'm warning you, the details of my story will add almost nothing to the version I gave you when I was first admitted.

As I told you, the night before we were locked up, Victor had gone out to a show put on by his agency, and I hadn't wanted to go with him. I rented a movie and ordered a couple of pizzas so I could enjoy the solitude I'd been craving, but that turned out to be impossible. Instead of relaxing, I spent the whole night dreading his return. The anxiety grew into a violent vertigo, and I rushed to the bathroom. When he got back, he found me hanging over the sink with the tweezers in hand. The reddish fleece all around me was proof of the massacre. I'd spent more than two hours extracting hairs indiscriminately and now displayed two big bald spots on top of my head.

"I can't stand it anymore!" he yelled when he saw me. There was alcohol on his breath. "For months, I've been dreaming of shaving your head." And when he said that, he punched the bathroom door hard with his closed fist. The blood that slid down his knuckles made me feel strangely relieved.

Maybe that night we were closer than ever to salvation, but we failed to identify the proper path, that is, a nice, hot cup of linden tea and then off to bed. It's always better to discuss important things in the morning. But we decided to take our usual route and called up our dealer. While we waited, I bandaged his injured hand, hoping he'd keep it covered for a long time.

We bought enough mescaline for three weeks and only left the house rarely, for food and water. During those three weeks, we somehow paid homage to our life together, listening to our records over and over again, showing each other photos that we'd never shared before. I discovered a six-year-old Rumanovich playing with snow on Lenin Square in Bucharest, and a fifteen-year-old one handing out Pizza Hut during anti-Communist demonstrations. He saw me very thin in my parents' house, next to my sister Luisa, with the beautiful tonsure of a monk and a face as strange as the one I had now, after several days spent smoking mescaline. The end was drawing near, and to avoid sitting down to cry, we kept taking that shit, which did nothing but accelerate the eruption of violence.

November 17

There are volcanoes that remain active for whole decades, for so long that one learns to live with their constant threat. I had always sensed a latent violence inside me, but it had never welled up into action, and I had even come to believe I knew how to contain it. I don't know if it was the mescal, the seclusion with Victor, or the photos from my childhood that coaxed it out, but one day, I couldn't stand it any longer. When you've lived your whole life in fear of one event, it inevitably arrives at the least opportune moment. It must have been around two in the afternoon. I was in the kitchen making a salad with artichokes and roasted red peppers for lunch. We had maintained the habit of eating something every day before smoking. From the kitchen window, I looked at the clear, beautiful sky and told myself that it would be a shame to spend yet another day inside the apartment. On the other hand, the drug was running out, and we had to decide if we were going to get more or stop for good. That's what I was thinking about when Victor showed up with a glass of whiskey in hand. His pajama pants had slipped down to his hips because of the weight he'd lost. He was leaning on the counter, using his good hand to play with the bits of lettuce I discarded. In a moment of despicable weakness, he bent his forefinger and cracked the two joints of his thumb right in my

face, the sound drilling into my brain. It was a reflex:
I shifted the course of the knife from the peppers and
thrust it toward his long fingers. Victor screamed. The
glass in his bandaged hand fell to the floor. When I saw
the blood spouting all over the place, my body cleverly
chose to lose consciousness. So he was forced to take
care of calling the ambulance and hiding the rest of
the mescaline with his bleeding hand. He didn't lose
any fingers, but they kept him in the hospital for a few
days to manage and cleanse the wound. Meanwhile, I
packed my bags and checked myself into this clinic.

November 23

Yesterday it was early in the morning, but it's happened
at other times, too. When I least expect it, I have the
feeling that Victor's cracklings have reached my room.
Is he still here, Doctor? If so, it would be best for us not
to see each other.

November 25

Last night, I forgot to take my medicine again. Isn't
it incredible, Doctor, how long we take to get used to
certain things? It takes us years to stop smoking or start
getting regular exercise, yet some habits slot into our

everyday lives the very first time. I'm thinking about
the woman the next room over: how long did it take
for her to acquire the tic of wrinkling her nose every
five minutes? And that gesture of yours, is it in response
to some emotion or thought you can't avoid? How is it
possible that one morning in my childhood—when I
discovered the tweezers on my mother's vanity table—
has dictated my existence to such an extent? Often,
while pulling my hair, I think about how hard it is
to free myself from this habit. It feels like it's always
existed, the same way an insect could never stop drinking from the pistil of the flowers his species has been
attracted to since the dawn of time. This will seem
crazy to you, Doctor, but in moments like this, I've
even gone so far as to believe in an infinity of previous
lives in which, irrevocably, I also pulled out my hair.

November 27

November has passed us by. I came to the clinic at the
beginning of October, and I won't leave until I'm finished with this story. I've made a date with Victor, out
on the cliff. One of us needs to go. Whatever happens,
I want to make it clear to my family—and to him, if
he survives—that I've always loved them and that it
was never my plan to hurt them, but that the habit
was stronger than all my good intentions. I thank my

parents for having put up with me, and I apologize to Victor for not having known how to put up with him. If I fail this afternoon in my attempt to free myself from him, I'm sure he'll be better off without my manias, that he'll end up admitting there's not room in this world for two people so similar, and he'll even feel some relief—the kind of relief he makes it impossible for me to experience. If I'm not finished off on the cliff, I'll stay here as long as is necessary. So now you understand that after all this, after all these years, I'm still looking for the same thing: the recipe for perfect calm.

About the Author

The New York Times described Guadalupe Nettel's acclaimed English language debut collection, *Natural Histories* (Seven Stories, 2014), as "five flawless stories." A Bogotá 39 author and *Granta* "Best Untranslated Writer," Nettel has received numerous prestigious awards, including the Gilberto Owen National Literature Prize, the Antonin Artaud Prize, the Ribera del Duero Short Fiction Award, and the 2014 Herralde Novel Prize. In 2015 Seven Stories published her first novel, *The Body Where I Was Born*. In 2018 her second novel, *After the Winter*, was published by Coffee House Press. Nettel lives and works in Mexico City.

About the Translator

Since the early 1970s SUZANNE JILL LEVINE has translated over forty volumes of Latin America's most innovative and distinguished fiction writers. The recipient of many honors, including several PEN awards, National Endowment for the Arts fellowships, and the Guggenheim Foundation Fellowship (for her literary biography of Manuel Puig), she edited for Penguin Classics in 2010 the five-volume series of Jorge Luis Borges's poetry and essays. Her translation of Luis Negron's *Mundo Cruel: Stories* (Seven Stories Press) received the Lambda Fiction Award in 2014, and most recently she co-translated Cristina Rivera Garza's *The Taiga Syndrome* (2018) for the Dorothy Project.